My Fair
GENTLEMAN

My Fair
GENTLEMAN

A PROPER ROMANCE

NANCY CAMPBELL ALLEN

SHADOW
MOUNTAIN

All rights reserved. No part of this book may be reproduced in any form or by any means without permission in writing from the publisher, Shadow Mountain®, at permissions@ shadowmountain.com. The views expressed herein are the responsibility of the author and do not necessarily represent the position of Shadow Mountain.

Visit us at ShadowMountain.com

This is a work of fiction. Characters and events in this book are products of the author's imagination or are represented fictitiously.

Library of Congress Cataloging-in-Publication Data
Allen, Nancy Campbell, 1969– author.
   My fair gentleman / Nancy Campbell Allen.
      pages cm
   ISBN 978-1-62972-095-1 (paperbound)
   1. Sailors—Fiction. I. Title.
   PS3551.L39644M9 2015
   813'.54—dc23   2015024110

Printed in the United States of America
Edwards Brothers Malloy, Ann Arbor, MI

10   9   8   7   6   5   4   3   2   1

To Mark, for hanging in there

And to Jen and Josi, sisters of my heart

CHAPTER 1

*It is ill-advised for gentlemen to be seen in places such
as taverns or gaming halls. It does little to aid the
reputation and can do much to harm it.*

Mistress Manners' Tips for Every-day Etiquette

Clarence Fuddleston, solicitor of the Earl of Stansworth's estate,
stood at the threshold of Tilly's Tavern and clutched his satchel
to his chest. He slowly removed his hat to reveal a balding head that
gleamed in the lamplight dancing just inside the door, and he pushed
his slipping round spectacles firmly up against the bridge of his nose.

Right, then.

Better to just get in, find the old earl's degenerate grandson, and
get out. With any luck he would be home within the hour and enjoying a warm spot of tea. The spring air was cold, colder still now that
dusk had given way to the dark of night, and the dockside was no
place a decent body wanted to spend an inordinate amount of time.
Not without a firearm at the ready, at any rate.

A lady—and he acknowledged the term should be applied
loosely—screeched in laughter as she poured a round of ale for the

1

group of rowdies closest to the door. Avoiding leers and inappropriate swats, she made her way around the table. She paused when she saw Clarence rooted to the spot.

"Ay, lovie, and are ya comin' in or not? It's a lot more where this came from," she said with a grin and hoisted the metal pitcher up in the air next to his face.

Clarence leaned away and cleared his throat. "If you please, madam, I am looking for someone in particular, a possible patron."

The woman's eyes narrowed a bit as she studied him, from the hat he held clenched in his fingers to the toes of his polished shoes. Tipping her head to one side, her gaze direct, she put one hand on her hip. "Whosit yer lookin' ta find? For some coin, I might be able ta point 'im out."

"I am searching for a man who goes by the name of 'Jack Elliot.' He is the first mate on Captain Stanley's merchant ship, the *Flying Gull*—the deckhands told me he frequents this eatery." Clarence resisted the urge to slip a finger between his collar and throat. If he hadn't so desperately needed the position with the old earl, he would have turned and walked quickly away from the tavern. A piano in the corner clinked loudly out of tune, and sailors laughed and argued with equal parts enthusiasm and volume. It was altogether uncouth and distasteful.

"Did ya 'ear 'im, boys? We're an 'eatery' now!" The woman looked over her shoulder and screeched again with laughter as Clarence felt his face redden.

"Here, then," he said, and he dug his hand into his trousers pocket. He withdrew a coin and thrust it at the woman. "Is Mr. Elliot here tonight?"

She took the money with a sly smile and jerked her head to the left. "Back in that corner be Jack. I shouldn't think ye'd want ta disturb 'im, though—up two 'ands, 'e is."

"Thank you," Clarence mumbled and stepped around the woman, who laughed again—directly in his ear—at a disparaging comment flung from the direction of the front table. He made his way through the crowded room, avoiding elbows and an occasional body as patrons shuffled, argued, and cackled at one another in debauched glee.

The farther into the bowels of the room he traveled, the more Clarence's vision was hampered by the dimming light. By the time he approached the far corner, he was forced to stop for a moment while his eyes adjusted to the darker shadows. When he was finally able to see clearly, he rather wished he couldn't.

It would be Stansworth's grandson there, no doubt about it. The same broad shoulders, the same facial features—defined jawline, sharply-angled planes, and fierce brows drawn together in a frown— why, the man even *sat* the same way. Perhaps the most glaring difference, however, was that the person before him was in the prime of health, if somewhat . . . slovenly. The old earl was on his deathbed. This man was nearing his thirtieth year and showing the glow of rigorous outdoor activity, while Clarence's employer was gray, racked with consumption, and fading quickly.

It was on that thought that Clarence composed himself and made his way to the object of his quest. "A word with you, Mr. Elliot," he said.

The seaman, dressed in a white shirt that had seen better days— open at the throat and grimy, no less—focused on the cards in his hand as one of the serving girls looked over his shoulder. "I do hope,

Vanessa, that you're not helping my opponent," Mr. Elliot said to the woman without looking up.

"Now, love, why would I do such a thing?" the girl demurred, although she did take a step back.

"Because he pays you to." Elliot finally looked up at the man seated across the table from him.

"That's a lie," the man growled. He rubbed a hand over his grizzled face and glared at Elliot. "Ye're callin' me a cheat!"

"Yes, I am." Jack Elliot tossed his cards faceup on the table and leaned back in his seat. "And even still, I win this hand."

Elliot's opponent stared at the table top for a moment, red color suffusing his complexion from his neck to the roots of his greasy hair. "Ye're the cheat!"

Elliot smiled; it wasn't a pleasant expression, and Clarence was glad to not be on the receiving end of it. "Never sit down to play cards with me again."

"Now, just a minute, 'ere. I'm not payin' you a farthin'!"

Jack Elliot leaned down slowly, and Clarence watched as he withdrew a thick, black, wicked-looking serrated knife from his boot. He quietly set the weapon on the table before him, never taking his eyes from his angry opponent.

The other man swallowed hard. His visage furious, he shoved the money sitting on the table in front of him toward Mr. Elliot and rose to leave, and Elliot motioned his head at the woman standing behind him. "You would be prudent to stay away from me as well," Elliot murmured to Vanessa, who scampered after the angry loser.

Clarence released his breath in a shaky whoosh, unaware he had been holding it. "Mr. Elliot," he said again, clearing his throat and inching closer. "I do require a moment of your time."

Jack Elliot finally looked up at him, meeting his gaze directly. "You lost, little man?"

"No, I am not los—" Clarence cut himself off and gestured to the now-empty chair across the table. "May I?" He was very near the end of his own rope and had endured all the insults to his dignity he would tolerate for one evening. Without waiting for Elliot's response, he sat in the chair and met his eyes. "Your grandfather sent me to find you."

Mr. Elliot smiled—again a cold mockery of a gentler emotion that Clarence was beginning to believe the sailor completely lacked. "You've got the wrong man. I don't have a grandfather."

Clarence opened his satchel and withdrew a single sheet of parchment—an official document written on the old earl's letterhead—and handed it to Elliot, who lifted one brow at him before reading it.

The man's expression never wavered and he didn't utter a word, so when he set the paper down carefully on the scarred wooden table and then stabbed the tip of his knife into the center of it, Clarence jumped, bumping his knees on the underside of the table.

"I believe I told you I do not have a grandfather." Elliot's voice was a quiet rumble yet audible even in the noise of the crowded tavern.

Clarence looked at the knife, which cleanly pierced the document, and then back up at the sailor. "But you do have a mother and sister, do you not?"

Jack Elliot's expression darkened, tightened, and Clarence forged bravely ahead, finally feeling as though he had the upper hand. "And although you provide for them as well as you can, the wages of a first mate on a merchant ship—even an experienced first mate—are still stretched thin in the face of insurmountable debt."

Elliot leaned forward and braced his elbows on the table. "My family is none of your affair, little worm, and if you come near me again I will dice you into pieces too small for even the fish to enjoy."

Clarence swallowed but persisted. "Your grandfather is on his deathbed," the solicitor said evenly, "and I am merely the messenger, sent to tell you that if you resist a meeting with the earl tomorrow morning at eight o'clock sharp, your mother's debts will come due in full immediately. The earl has purchased them."

Jack Elliot was still, those striking eyes watchful and his entire demeanor nearly predatory as a muscle in his jaw twitched. Once.

"I urge you to keep the appointment, Mr. Elliot. I sincerely doubt either of us wishes for me to set foot in this establishment ever again." Clarence nodded at the paper impaled on the tabletop. "The address is there on the letterhead."

And on trembling legs, Clarence Fuddleston rose from the table and shoved his way out of the tavern. Pausing at the door to place his hat on his head, he stepped out into the cold night air.

CHAPTER 2

When ladies and gentlemen call on their elders,
great care should be taken to treat them with the utmost
respect. As they age, they grow ever feebler and require
decorum and gentle words of affection. One would be
well-advised to recite poetry—Shelley or Keats, perhaps.

Mistress Manners' Tips for Every-day Etiquette

Jack Elliot donned his cleanest shirt and breeches, barely resist-ing the impulse to wear his dirtiest outfit, which hadn't seen soap or water for over eight weeks. He couldn't stand the smell himself, though, and it would be sad indeed if he were more adversely affected by the stench than the old man was. He didn't bother polishing his boots, which had survived two months at sea, and he squelched the suggestion, cheekily offered by his cabin boy, of wearing a coat.

"I am not dressing to impress," Jack told Pug, standing before the small mirror in his proportionately small cabin aboard the *Flying Gull*. "I am going to set the man straight and will return by nine o'clock. Half past, at the latest."

Pug Smith—scruffy, twelve years old, and tall for his age, shook his head. "Don't make sense, walkin' away from a fortune."

Jack scowled at the boy and motioned toward the door. "When

I return, I expect to see the laundry well under way," he told Pug as he locked the cabin door behind them. "No excuses this time, or I'll throw you overboard."

Pug snorted. "If you threw me overboard half as much as you threaten it, I'd never get dry!"

Jack held back a smile, but only just. It wouldn't do for the little urchin to see he had a soft spot. "And once you hang the clothes to dry, complete two full pages in the arithmetic primer. I'll review it this afternoon."

The answering whine was predictable—Pug was nothing if not consistent. "I hate it! I will never have a use for it. My mum doesn't know if I do it or don't!"

"I promised her I would teach you." Jack held up a hand when the boy opened his mouth to continue. "And you did visit her last night, as I suggested?"

"'Suggested,'" the boy sulked. "*Commanded*. You don't 'suggest' anything."

"And?"

Pug snorted. "I saw her. Same old shack, same noisy brats, new man to smack her about the head and shoulders."

Jack tensed but refrained from further comment. Pug had an ingrained sense of responsibility for his mother—very much like the feeling Jack himself had possessed when he'd signed on as cabin boy with a merchant ship at ten years of age. The year his father had died and left them not only penniless but under a heaping mound of debt.

"Remember, wash the clothing—yours also—and then do your mathematics," Jack told him as they reached the gangplank. "If it's not done, I'll—"

"Throw me overboard, I know." Pug's expression was heavy, and Jack wished it were only because the boy didn't want to do his work.

"Was there food in the house?"

Pug shrugged. "Enough."

Jack looked at the boy for a moment before turning to make his way off the ship. "I don't imagine it would be an enjoyable way to spend an afternoon—in the water with the sharks," he called over his shoulder. He didn't look to see the boy's reaction, but he hoped his parting shot had at least brought forth an exasperated roll of the eyes. The boy carried the weight of his young world on his shoulders.

Once he reached the docks, Jack hailed a passing hack and climbed in, giving the driver the Mayfair address. The driver gave him a quick appraising glance but remained wisely silent. As he settled back into the uncomfortably worn seat, Jack closed his eyes for a moment and wondered what was happening to his well-ordered world.

He had grown up at sea—had even been impressed into naval service for two years—and was now mere months away from captaining a merchant vessel of his own. He had clawed and scraped his way through the years to achieve his current status, and now, with the stroke of a pen, his blasted grandfather had set in motion wheels that might well derail all of his hard work.

The streets were an assault on the senses. He never quite forgot how it felt to be a child with a newly deceased father, begging for the smallest scraps of food. The sight of the street urchins stirred memories he would much prefer to leave long buried, but his gut clenched anyway, and he felt a stab of pain when he recognized himself in their gaunt faces. His mother had cried the day he'd left to be a cabin boy; his only consolation had been that with him away, she had one less mouth to feed.

The ride to the earl's town house was, regrettably, not nearly long enough for Jack's liking, and the fact that he'd had to relive snippets of his childhood propelled a dark mood into a black one. He glanced at his pocket watch as the vehicle came to a stop in front of the house, disappointed to see that he was two minutes early. He had wanted to be late, merely to prove a point. He supposed his dingy appearance alone would have to suffice. He did possess one nice suit, but he had decided—as he was finally falling asleep after that meeting in the tavern with the little toad—that he would not show any kind of respect for the old man who had ruined his life before Jack had even drawn his first breath. It was only personal pride that had kept him from showing up hungover, with bloodshot eyes and alcohol on his breath.

Finally deciding he couldn't avoid the inevitable, he paid the cab driver and made his way to the front door. It was a large, beautiful home on a beautiful street, and he hated it on sight. Raising the door knocker with a fair amount of distaste, he rapped sharply and waited.

"Yes?"

Jack eyed the stoic butler through the slightly opened door and, with an effort, tamped down the anger rising in his chest. "My name is Jack Elliot. I'm here at the request of . . ." He choked on the words, couldn't spit them out.

"His Lordship, the Earl of Stansworth?" the butler intoned.

Jack nodded once and felt his nostrils flare with expressed air.

"His Lordship is expecting you. This way, if you please." Jack entered the foyer and endured the butler's quick perusal. "I would offer to take your hat and coat, but . . ."

Jack shot a look at the man, who stood a good foot shorter than his own six feet two. "But I'm not wearing either," he said flatly, maintaining eye contact until the butler looked away.

The man had enough sense to refrain from further comment and instead led Jack up a wide staircase that turned on a landing and then continued the rest of the way to the second floor. Jack took in his surroundings as they traveled the length of a long hallway, well aware that they should have been familiar to him. The house should have been one in which he'd spent countless hours as a child, running from nannies and being scolded for causing a ruckus in his grandparents' home.

He looked at the high ceilings, the crisp mouldings, the plants placed on side tables and at the end of the hallway beneath a cleaned and polished window that looked as if it had only just been installed and painted. He tried to envision his father walking that very hall and couldn't draw forth the image. It was difficult to remember him clearly, though. Twenty years had done much to dull the memory.

Finally, at the last door on the right, the butler stopped and knocked once, lightly, before opening it a crack. Jack heard a response from inside the room, and the door opened wider to reveal the little toad.

"Clarence Fuddleston." The man bowed slightly. "We met last night."

Jack looked down at him for a moment before finally responding. "I remember," he said drily. He stepped into the room and, in spite of his best intentions, allowed his eyes to wander until he saw the object of his frustrations. The large doors leading from the dressing room to his grandfather's bedchamber were wide open.

"Come here, then," his grandfather said from the bed, where he sat propped against a mountain of pillows. Fuddleston hadn't exaggerated; the old man seemed to be knocking at death's door as they stood there. As if reading his thoughts, the solicitor gave him a look of . . .

what? Sympathy? Fuddleston beckoned in invitation and followed when Jack finally made his feet move across the thick carpet and into the bedchamber.

Jack looked at his grandfather, not bothering to hide the distaste he knew was written on his face. He had to admit, grudgingly, that the old earl had probably once looked very much like Jack's father, and in fact Jack himself would likely resemble the old man when it was his turn to die, if fate decreed he should live that long.

The earl's eyes clouded then, and Jack was relieved to find himself unmoved. "You are the very vision of your father," Stansworth said.

"A fact you might have known if you had bothered to look for us through the years."

The earl gestured to a chair that had been placed by the bedside. "Sit."

"I prefer to stand."

The earl coughed, the spasm overtaking him quickly, and he hacked into a handkerchief he clutched in his bony fingers. When he pulled it away from his mouth, it was liberally smeared with red, and he hastily folded it in half with hands that shook. "I didn't have to look for you," he said, his voice like gravel. He gestured toward a glass of water on the nightstand. Jack, seeing that he stood between the nightstand and Fuddleston, finally reached for the glass himself and handed it to the old man.

The earl swallowed the sip of water and cleared his throat, as winded as if he had run a mile. "I knew where you were the whole time," he continued. "I kept myself abreast of your comings and goings; I was even at David's funeral."

"You have no right to speak his name." Jack kept his voice even, pleased that it didn't vibrate with the anger he was sure must be rolling off him in waves.

"He was my son."

"Whom you disinherited. I do not have time for idle chitchat. Tell me what you want for my mother's debts and we will finish this ridiculous charade."

The earl smiled. "Smart you are, well-spoken. It is in your blood." He coughed again. "Your mother's debts are more than you can pay, even now. Even as you are about to claim your own ship. The price for your mother's debts is as I wrote in the letter to you: You take your place as my heir and accept the earldom when I die."

"My father wasn't your heir, and neither am I."

"I've had the documents processed." Stansworth broke into another coughing fit. The sound was horrid, and Jack took perverse satisfaction in the notion that the one who had been responsible for so much misery was now meeting a painful end.

Jack felt the fragile tether he held on his patience begin to tear as he fully processed his grandfather's statement. *He'd already had the documents processed?* "Why?" he ground out. "Why now? You cast out my father because he dared to marry a fisherman's daughter and then suddenly decide you want *her* son to take your place?" He rubbed the back of his neck at the base of his skull—a fall from the ship's rigging when he was a cabin boy had inflicted an injury that still throbbed when he was under stress. He caught himself and forced his hand back to his side, unwilling to show weakness or any sign of agitation.

"My late brother's son—your father's cousin Percival—is the next in line." The earl leaned back against the pillows, looking even more pale and drawn than when Jack had entered. "And he is an idiot. I will not have him in this home, bearing my title. I will see it passed to my own direct line before I die."

"I do not want it. I am finished—have Mr. Fussbottom here begin the process to change the documents. I will find another way to repay the debt. You find yourself another heir." Jack turned and elbowed his way past the solicitor, who looked at him with wide eyes.

"Your sister, Sophia, she is a ladies' maid, is she not?" the old man said.

Jack stopped cold. "Leave her alone," he growled. He turned slowly on his heel.

"Nineteen years old, prettier than any of the ladies she's had the misfortune to wait upon. As is always evidenced by the unwanted attention of the master of the house. She's quickly running short of options—isn't she? Entirely innocent though she is, there aren't many ladies left in town willing to hire her, and if she were to lose her current position, I fear she would be forced into a drudge's work, or worse. Whitechapel is full of young women who have no choices left."

"If you were not already so close to death, I would hasten you there myself." Jack felt a vein in his forehead throbbing. Indeed, it was all he could do to keep from vaulting up onto the bed and strangling the life out of the earl.

"I can make things very pleasant for your family with a nod to my solicitor here. Would you like to hear the terms?"

Jack's hand found the back of his neck by itself and massaged the ache there that he knew would develop into full-blown, debilitating pain within the hour. "What terms?"

"You relinquish your position as first mate aboard the *Flying Gull* and take up residence here immediately. By evening, I will have your mother and sister moved to a home less than a mile away from here that has already been secured and furnished for their arrival. I have an account established in their names that will pay them yearly from the estate—neither of them need work another day in their lives. This would be especially good for your mother, who seems susceptible to every illness that makes its way through her sewing clientele."

Jack's heart thumped in his chest. He hadn't known . . . his mother had never said anything. She had always been thin; he knew the London air couldn't be good for her, but weak, even ill? How had he not known? Feeling slightly sick, he fought to keep from bracing himself against the huge bed's four-post frame. The silence that roared through the room was deafening.

"Why would it be so horrible?" the old man finally asked, quiet and weary. "To be titled, with money beyond your wildest expectations, and your family well-provided for throughout the rest of their lives?"

"Because it's *yours*." Jack met his eyes, hating the very sight of him. "My father worked his fingers to the bone, and it still wasn't enough. He borrowed from creditors who had no intentions of ever setting him free, and in the end he died on the docks.

"I went to sea as a *child* to provide for my mother, who had a new baby and no income, when I should have been living in a warm home, with both of my parents, not knocked around and abused by deckhands who had nothing better to amuse them."

"It has made you strong," the earl wheezed, coughing.

The earl was once again orchestrating events to meet his own desires, and it felt like a noose around Jack's neck. And yet the threat was clear—follow the man's directives, or Jack's family would suffer horribly. He had absolutely no choice. He felt heated with the restraint it took to keep from tearing the room apart with his hands.

"Your actions killed my father and nearly destroyed my mother," he hissed at the old man. "I hope that when you leave this room, you find yourself in hell." Jack turned, glancing at Fuddleston as he made his way to the door. "Give the orders," he told the shorter man. "I want my mother and sister in that house by sundown."

CHAPTER 3

*It is always a pleasure to help those in need, especially as
it concerns proper behavior and decorum; when a lady or
gentleman is given an opportunity to instruct or lead by example,
it is an honour to be executed with a smile upon one's face.*

Mistress Manners' Tips for Every-day Etiquette

I vy Carlisle's brow knit in a frown. A delicate frown, but a frown
nonetheless. "Nana, I'm not altogether certain that one month is
enough time to teach a sailor proper behavior. Especially if he has, as
you say, spent the bulk of his life aboard a ship in the consistent company of ruffians. Were he a military man, it would be infinitely easier,
of course, but his experience is with *merchant* vessels."

Olivia Knightley Carlisle, dowager countess of Huntington,
smiled at her granddaughter over her cup of tea. "He did serve two
years in His Majesty's Royal Navy. Perhaps the task will not be as
daunting as it seems. At any rate, his grandmother was my dearest friend in my youth, and I've made a promise to her dying husband that I will do my best to see the grandson launched into polite
society."

Ivy frowned again and took a bite of her fruit salad, chewing it carefully as she registered the familiar feel of the dining room that had been the site of her weekly luncheon with Nana for as long as she could remember. The servants moved gracefully, almost silently. Manners were observed to perfection; all was appropriate and familiar. Comfortable.

And now Nana wanted her to instruct a merchant seaman in the ways of polite society? It might be too difficult a task for even the accomplished Lady Ivy Carlisle to manage. But then, she never had been one to back down from a challenge.

"Ivy," Nana said, wiping at the corner of her mouth with a linen napkin, "you could do with a little something out of the ordinary. Do you not ever wish for more variety in the day?"

"I have plenty of variety." Ivy felt suddenly defensive. The last time Nana had broached a conversation of this sort, Ivy had found herself submitting a sample advice column to *The Fine Lady's Weekly Journal*, which, to her surprise, had met with success. She had thought her weekly contribution to the ladies' magazine—although written under the unidentifiable pseudonym of "Mistress Manners"—would have quieted her grandmother on the subject of Ivy's supposedly boring life.

"I speak not of a succession of afternoon teas and evening soirees, giving advice and teaching decorum to debutantes approaching the Season." The older woman leaned in a bit, her eyes sparkling. "Do you never want to cause a bit of a scandal, Ivy?"

Ivy felt her eyes widen. "Nana!" She glanced over her shoulder, hoping the servants had not overheard. "You know very well I cannot afford to step a foot out of line after Caroline's disgrace," she whispered.

Nana shook her head. "I am not suggesting you run off to the continent with a soldier who has abandoned his regiment. Something milder. Dance the waltz three times with the same gentleman in one evening. Or be fitted for breeches and learn to ride astride rather than sidesaddle."

"Nana," Ivy sighed, "you are destined to be this family's only Original. You are able to do and say things the rest of us cannot." She scowled, knowing full well the wrinkles such an expression would produce over time. "I am a writer now—for *pay*, no less—at your prodding. I had rather hoped the subject of my 'daring' would be closed."

Lady Carlisle took another sip of her tea and studied Ivy for so long that the young woman felt the urge to squirm. If she had been the kind to squirm, of course. "There is much in life to enjoy," Nana finally said quietly. "Ivy, it wasn't so long ago that you bubbled over with joy; it was infectious. And your temper was as enthusiastic as was your happiness. You still have that fiery personality beneath your calm exterior, and I curse the day your sister ruined her own life and squelched the spirit in yours."

Ivy felt a stab of sadness but refused to acknowledge it. "You know it very nearly killed my parents. I will not be responsible for causing the family name an ounce of disgrace." She fought hard enough for their approval as it was.

Nana's expression tightened fractionally, but she refrained from comment. Ivy found herself wondering what the older woman was thinking, but she decided it was probably better for her not to know.

"Now, then, this merchant sailor." Ivy's tone was brisk. "Whose grandson is he?"

"Lord Stansworth's."

Ivy's mouth dropped open for a moment, and she clamped it shut. "But the earl disinherited his son and family years ago."

"And he is now dying and wishes for his own direct bloodline to carry on the title."

"I suspect Lord Percival has much to say on the subject."

Nana grimaced. "He may indeed, but it is of no consequence. In fact, he no longer retains the title of 'Lord.' He has been officially written out, and John Elliot written in. I understand he goes by the name 'Jack.'"

"At sea, perhaps. He shall have to familiarize himself with his given name if this is going to work. Nobody is going to take him seriously as an earl with the name of 'Jack.'"

Nana's lips twitched.

"What is it?" Ivy finished the last of her meal and aligned the silverware neatly on her plate to indicate to the servants that she was finished. "Why are you laughing?"

"I'm not laughing at all. So, you are agreeing, then? You'll take him on as a client, of sorts?"

Ivy frowned. "I suppose so, although we shan't call him a 'client.' Mother would think it vulgar if I were to have clients."

Nana muttered something under her breath, but Ivy missed it. "I'm sorry?"

"Nothing." Nana smiled brightly as she stood up. "We had best be on our way to the earl's home. Mr. Elliot should be there—he met with Stansworth yesterday and agreed to the stipulations."

"And what were those?" Ivy asked as they made their way to the door.

"I'm not certain, although Fuddleston insinuated that Mr. Elliot was less than enthused about his future."

Ivy's bafflement knew no bounds thirty minutes later when she stood with Mr. Fuddleston in the earl's second-floor receiving room that adjoined the bedroom. "He's not here?" Ivy asked. "Well, where is he?"

Fuddleston rubbed a hand across his balding head and looked at her through round spectacles that gave him rather the appearance of an owl. His cravat was slightly askew, and a sheen of perspiration glistened on his upper lip. "I do not know," the short man said through gritted teeth. He wasn't much taller than Ivy's five foot two, but in his present mood, she didn't imagine an encounter in a dark alley would be a pleasant one. Although what one might be doing in a dark alley, she could hardly fathom.

The solicitor shook his head. "I sent a note early this morning that Mr. Elliot's attendance was requested at the earl's bedside. We haven't seen hide nor hair of him, and I must go back in there." He motioned to the door, through which Ivy's grandmother had gone the moment they had arrived.

"Why not send a messenger or footman?"

Fuddleston glanced at her askance. "I'm afraid Mr. Elliot would send such a person flying on his ear."

Ivy pursed her lips. *Wonderful.* Mr. Elliot was already proving to be difficult, and she hadn't even met the man yet! He needed to be at his grandfather's bedside—at least in the house, for heaven's sake. What sort of man was this, really?

"You go in," she told Fuddleston. "My grandmother will keep you company, and I shall fetch Mr. Elliot."

Fuddleston shook his head. "Your grandmother hardly needs to remain at his Lordship's bedside. He will pass at any time—it really is rather ghastly."

"Lady Olivia Carlisle does as she pleases. I would imagine she is right now issuing instructions for the earl to pass along her love to his deceased wife when he crosses to the other side. You needn't worry on her account. And as for Mr. Elliot—is he aware that I am to instruct him in manners and decorum? That is, the sight of me will not be altogether unexpected?"

"I . . . Lady Ivy . . . you should know that Mr. Elliot is quite, can be quite, that is . . ."

Ivy waved a hand in the air. "Mr. Fuddleston, if you were to search for Mr. Elliot, where would you begin?"

The small man looked at her for a long moment and then started a bit at the sound of a harsh cough on the other side of the door. "I suppose I would begin at his ship, the *Flying Gull.* It's in dock for another two days. Lady Ivy, it is unseemly, you simply cannot go there."

"I shall take Nana's footman with me. He is very large and strong. And one of your maids will do fine. I would fetch my own lady's maid but I worry we will not have time." Ivy winced at the racking coughing noise that carried out from the bedchamber.

Fuddleston nodded and turned, leading her back downstairs and introducing her to Mrs. Harster, the housekeeper. Mrs. Harster was pale and flustered—the master of the house did not die every day, of course, and they had a new master set to take up residence at any time. Provided he could be accounted for.

"Millie," Mrs. Harster said to a young woman who dashed by with a feather duster. "You must accompany Lady Ivy Carlisle on an errand."

Millie stopped midstride and spun around, her eyes wide. "Me?"

she squeaked, a bright smile crossing her face as she bobbed a quick curtsey to Ivy. Her soft red hair curled becomingly under her white cap and framed her face. "Oh, bless you, Mrs. Harster. I have got to get out of this house!"

"Millie!"

Ivy smiled at the housekeeper. "These are trying times, Mrs. Harster. A little uncertainty is to be expected."

Mille raised a brow. "Boredom is more like it." She handed the duster to the housekeeper, who gaped at the girl.

"Come, then," Ivy said and made her way to the door as Millie skipped to catch up. "And how long have you been in the earl's employ?"

"Only but a week, and the longest week of my life, too! My mum knew Mrs. Harster, and when there was a vacancy come open I was given the position, even though I'm younger than Mrs. Harster likes."

Ivy accepted her light pelisse from the butler and started out the door as Millie dashed below stairs for her own wrap. "And have you had much training, then?" Ivy asked Millie as the girl clambered up into the waiting carriage behind her.

"Some, I s'pose. Mrs. Harster, though, she's been frightful distracted. What with his Lordship ready to keel over and all."

Ivy glanced at Millie and then turned to give the footman quick instructions. As she and the young maid settled into the carriage, Ivy gave her a long look and fought the twitch trying desperately to escape the corners of her mouth. "Millie, we are strangers, you and I. It is hardly the thing for you to refer in such a crass way to your employer's demise. I might suggest that if you wish to maintain your post, you should consider practicing a bit more professional decorum."

Millie blinked at her with wide, expressive eyes that clearly stated she had no experience with professional decorum. Ivy wondered why she bothered lecturing the girl—it wasn't as though she was a member of the household, and even as the words had come out of her mouth, Ivy had registered the fact that she was sounding—how did Nana sometimes put it? Bossy.

Ivy smiled at the girl. "You just do your very best. Follow instructions and behave with respect."

Millie bobbed her head in agreement. "I can do that. My mum told me that his Lordship is frightful hideous, bein' old and almost dead, but that I wasn't ta mention it. What with him payin' my wages and all."

Ivy paused and bit the inside of her cheek. "That is very sound advice," she finally said. "Your mother must be a wise woman indeed."

The carriage bumped and bounced over the streets—some well paved, others not—and finally came to a stop some time later. The sound of seagulls was loud, and the smell of the waterfront lifted on the wind to enter the conveyance and announce their arrival at the docks. As Ivy climbed down from the carriage and squinted at the ships lined in the harbor, she shielded her hand against the sun and reached back into the carriage for her parasol.

"Which one is it, then, Albert?" Ivy asked the footman as she snapped the parasol open.

"That 'un there, I b'lieve, my lady." Albert looked at a ship directly before them in some consternation and scratched at his head beneath his hat. "Yer sure 'bout this?"

Now that Ivy stood in the flesh before the massive vessel, she wasn't sure about anything. Squaring her shoulders, she remembered her grandmother's attitude at luncheon and stiffened her resolve. Lady Ivy Carlisle could do brave things. She could do anything, in fact, as long as it wasn't inappropriate. Granted, visiting a bachelor—a sailor, no less—on a merchant vessel was far from appropriate, but desperate times called for desperate measures. And the cause was sound.

"Right, then," she murmured and began walking toward the gangplank. "Millie, Albert, we must take Mr. Elliot with us back to the earl's home. We're not leaving without him."

CHAPTER 4

When making a new acquaintance, always present
a pleasant face and a kindly manner.

Mistress Manners' Tips for Every-day Etiquette

"here's what here to see me?" Jack asked Pug, who stood inside the cabin doorway with a bewildered expression.

"Someone—a lady—says she's here to take you back to Stansworth House."

"What the devil," Jack cursed and threw an armload of personal objects into his trunk. He'd said his farewells earlier in the day to his shipmates, and he had already spent a fair amount of time the night before with his captain, complaining about his lot and attempting to drown his sorrows in stiff drink. All it had gotten him was a blazing headache and a shorter fuse.

"Let her in, then," Jack said over his shoulder to Pug, who finally turned with a shrug. The boy returned moments later with a delicate vision of loveliness in a light spring dress and a beribboned and lacy bonnet. She had no business being dockside, let alone aboard the

Flying Gull. A young maid and tall footman hovered just outside the cramped cabin in the equally cramped companionway.

This should be most interesting.

Jack straightened to his full height and had the momentary satisfaction of seeing his guest's eyes widen slightly before she recovered herself and managed a smile.

"Mr. Elliot, then?" She stepped forward and extended her gloved hand. "I'm Lady Ivy Carlisle, daughter of the Duke and Duchess of Huntington, and I have been asked by your grandfather to . . . to . . ."

"Make a gentleman out of me?" he said flatly.

"Well, I'm certain you are already well on your way," she said and swallowed visibly. "Perhaps you might benefit from a few tips and suggestions. I understand your formal launch into Society will occur at a ball once the Season is in full swing in one month's time."

The lady was smooth; he would give her that much. She was clearly nervous but managed to deliver her little speech with all the polish he would expect of a person of quality. It irritated him no end.

"Why are you here right now, Miss Carlisle? Were you under the impression that my lessons are to begin immediately?" He deliberately dropped her title and wondered if it would cause her to swoon.

She flushed. "No. That is . . ." She straightened her shoulders and met his eyes squarely. "Mr. Elliot, your grandfather is, as we speak, nearly breathing his last. It is most unseemly for you to be away from his bedside at such a time."

Jack folded his arms, feeling his eyelid twitch. "As I am hopeful my grandfather's soul will burn eternally, the last thing I care about in this world right now is being at that man's bedside while he 'breathes his last.'" His words were proper enough, he knew, but he deliberately accented them with the rough edge one might expect of a sailor.

Lady Ivy's mouth had dropped open, and she quickly shut it. "Mr. Elliot, I have been charged with easing you into your new position as the Earl of Stansworth, and it begins now. Today. If you intend for people to accept you as your grandfather's heir, you must begin acting the part. It will be that much harder on you if Society learns that when the old earl was dying, his grandson lounged around his merchant ship down by the docks."

"Miss Carlisle, I don't give a flying fig for what Society thinks of me."

"And yet you have a mother and sister, do you not? Are you willing to drag them down into the dregs with you? I should think you would have a care for their welfare."

He wouldn't have believed it possible, but the little woman had shut him up. She'd found his Achilles' heel. He felt a surge of anger and welcomed it. "You will leave my mother and sister out of this."

"I would love to, sir—however, the rest of the *ton* will not. You no longer have the luxury of expecting that your behavior will affect only you."

The silence between them stretched into several long moments before she spoke again. "Mr. Elliot," she said quietly, "the old man is dying, and you are to take his place. I understand you've agreed to it and I urge you to follow my lead. I'll torture you for only four weeks' time, after which you need never lay eyes on me again. Well," she amended, "I expect you might; we will be moving in the same circles, after all, but you needn't lay eyes on me for very long. You can turn your head if you see me coming." She offered that last with a small smile. He imagined she had disarmed many an opponent with that smile. And, drat it all, her reasoning was sound.

Agreed to it, she had said. He had not so much agreed as been blackmailed into it. But what was done was done, and the old man's orders would haunt Jack even from beyond the grave. If Jack were to step down or turn the earldom over to another, his mother and sister would find themselves homeless and in more of a mess than they'd been before. He ground his teeth and refrained from picking up the nearest object not tacked down and hurling it through the porthole.

"I am finished here," he finally growled, stooping beside his trunk to close and lock it.

"Are there any to whom you should bid farewell?" Ivy asked him, her pretty brow marred by a light frown.

"I don't suppose it matters much, now, does it?" he threw back at the woman. "My mother and sister will face fates worth than death if I do not come with you right this very instant."

For the briefest flash, he saw something cross the lady's face: irritation? Anger? It was in the subtle, nearly imperceptible flare of her nostrils and thinning of her lips—and it was gone almost before it was even there. Perhaps the lady had a temper. Well, that was fine with him. She was making his life miserable; he ought to at least return the favor.

Jack hefted his trunk and followed the woman out of his cabin, looking back one last time before he closed the door. "You have your things ready?" he said to his cabin boy.

Pug nodded and picked up a satchel that carried all of his worldly possessions.

"My valet," he said to Ivy as she regarded the boy in some surprise. "This is Pug, and he will be joining us."

"P-P-Pug?" Ivy looked at Jack with wide eyes and then back at the boy.

Jack found himself suddenly very defensive of his young charge. "Yes. Pug."

"Very well, then," she said with a smile, and he had to wonder if it was forced. "Millie. Albert." She turned and led the entourage down the narrow companionway, and he felt a knot of dread form deep in his gut. Uncharted waters lay before him, and he didn't relish the prospect of sailing into them.

CHAPTER 5

Apparel is most crucial in creating the proper impression.
While items must not be so costly as to cause consternation
to the allotted budget, attention should always be paid
to creating the best impression possible.

Mistress Manners' Tips for Every-day Etiquette

Ivy entered the earl's library early the next morning with a firm purpose and a list in hand. The old earl had died in the night, and the house was officially in mourning and preparing for a funeral. The new earl, John Weldon Elliot, was in the act of being fitted for a suit coat, and he didn't look in the least pleased about it. "Excellent," she said briskly and set her reticule on a side table. "There is one item on the list we can cross off already." She gave the man a healthy smile and kept it firmly fixed when he scowled at her in return.

"I have a coat upstairs," he grumbled with a glare at the elderly tailor, Mr. Pearson, who paid the earl little mind, measuring every possible angle of the man's torso, chest, shoulders, and arms.

Ivy raised a brow. "I'm sure you do. I am also certain that it will not do justice to the events the next several weeks will bring. You are now an earl and must dress the part." She circled around to the side and observed the measuring with a slight nod. "You note, of course, the width across the shoulders," she said to Mr. Pearson. "He does seem a bit broader than most."

"Of course, my lady," Mr. Pearson intoned, adjusting his spectacles and draping the measuring tape around his neck. He made notations in a small notebook as he continued his perusal of the sailor-turned-gentleman.

Mr. Elliot, for she was having a difficult time of it thinking of him as the earl, shot her a flat look. "I apologize for inconveniencing you," he said.

"Now, now," Ivy said as she circled back around to stand before him, "no need at all to be nasty, my lord."

"My name is Jack."

"To your mother, perhaps."

The man's nostrils flared, and his jaw visibly clenched. "I am being measured for a wardrobe I do not want and addressed by a title I do not desire. Miss Carlisle, you mistake my relative calm for patience, which I can assure you I possess in very limited supply."

"And how glad I am you tap into those limited reserves, my lord. Might I also suggest, however, that you take pains to deepen the well. If the next four weeks are to be met with success on any level, you will likely need it." She turned her attention back to the tailor. "Mr. Pearson, has his Lordship been fitted for the rest of his wardrobe already?"

"His Lordship has indeed," the earl interrupted. "Poked, prodded, and generally abused. We came down here to finish only because you sent word you were on your way, and skinny man, here, thought it prudent that you be neither kept waiting nor entertained in my dressing room or bedchamber."

Ivy looked at the earl with what she hoped was equanimity, all the while noting the shocked expression of the tailor in her periphery. Fighting a blush by thinking of bland things—like porridge without a dash of sugar—she refrained from delivering a blistering diatribe on the earl's outlandish comment. "You are new to this position, my lord, and therefore will be afforded a certain degree of allowance for inappropriate remarks. You'll find that certain things are not to be mentioned in polite company—the words 'entertained' and 'bedchamber' most especially should not be used in the same breath. It will be considered shocking."

"And if that was my intention? I can assure you, rarely do I misspeak."

Ivy tipped her head to one side, struck for a moment at the incongruity between what she knew of his past and his delivery. "You are well-spoken, my lord, come to think of it. Although your pronunciation marks you clearly as one of the working class."

He rested a look upon her that she decided would be best not to interpret.

"Perhaps this task will not be as daunting as I had supposed."

Mr. Elliot cocked a brow. "You were expecting an oaf."

"I can only judge that which I have observed." Ivy fought the urge to clap her hand over her mouth, hoping that her quick retort was not an omen of things to come. She was not usually so blunt. Or cutting.

"Well, well." The new earl smiled at her, but there was no warmth behind it. "The mistress of manners has some bite."

Ivy gaped at him, wondering for a fleeting moment how he might know she wrote as "Mistress Manners." Realizing it had just been a coincidence, she flushed. Things weren't going well at all. The silence in the room stretched, and the earl made no attempt to ease the discomfort. Mr. Pearson finished his measurements and, with a few final scribbles in his notebook, packed up his bag, bowed slightly, and left the room.

Taking her courage firmly in hand, Ivy straightened her spine and forced a smile. "I have an itinerary of your lessons we must review. And the sooner the better, as the funeral is nearly upon us."

The earl was quiet for a moment, eyeing her with a blank expression that gave nothing away, and finally indicated a pair of chairs before the fireplace. "Be on with it, then," he said and sank into one of the seats.

Ivy remained standing. "You must not take a seat before a lady does." It was the most elementary item of etiquette, and he was totally ignorant of it? Perhaps she'd not been mistaken, and training the man would be every bit the chore she had imagined at the outset.

The earl stood, made a sweeping gesture with his hand, and locked his eyes with hers until she sat down across from him. "If you would be so kind as to allow me to sit now?"

She nodded. "I can see that we must begin with basics," she said as he took his seat and pinched the bridge of his nose between his thumb and forefinger, his eyes closed. "My lord? Are you ill?"

He opened his eyes and regarded her with a stare that had likely rattled the fortitude of many a lowly sailor. They had precious little time, however, and she steeled her resolve, determined to accomplish her objective.

"The funeral is regrettably soon, of course. Thankfully, nobody will be expecting you to say or do much. Simply be in attendance and make an effort to speak as little as possible. Your words are usually fine, but the delivery is, well, rough."

He watched her with eyes at half-mast. "So I'm little more than an idiot monkey boy. Why don't we just invite all of London to come and gawk at me in a cage? I'll do my best to keep my mouth shut."

Ivy took a deep breath. "Mr. . . . my lord, I certainly intended no insult. But you must understand, the stakes in this endeavor are very high indeed. If we cannot present you well, it will affect your sister and mother in a way most unpleasant. I am hoping to meet with them soon to assess their needs."

The jaw tightened visibly again, and Lord Stansworth leaned forward, ever so slightly. "My mother and sister are exceptionally well mannered, and I'll not have them treated like street trash."

"As if I would do so!" Ivy's temper flared and she muscled it back into submission. "My lord, you do not know me in the slightest, but I must have your trust in these matters. I am kind, and I intend for these transitions to be smooth and seamless for your family. I understand they are undergoing a huge amount of upheaval, and although I would certainly consider the changes in their circumstances to be an improvement, variance from a routine can be difficult."

Ivy paused and regarded the man sitting opposite her, cold and defensive, with hostility roiling just beneath the surface. To her surprise, she felt a stab of pity. "I want very much for your loved ones to succeed. It's true, you've been at sea all these long years, but you must know how cruel Society can be," she said, her voice soft.

"I am thinking of sending them to live at the country estate," the earl admitted gruffly. He stared into the flames of the fire. "I will not have them mocked."

Ivy sighed. He truly didn't understand the impact his new status would have on his family. "Do you consider your mother and sister to be of the intelligent sort?"

He looked back at her with a scowl. "Of course I do."

"Then you must allow them the opportunity to succeed in this environment. And your sister is young yet and deserves a season or two of her own. I should think you would want her to make a good match."

"I'll not force her to marry some old codger against her will."

"But you'll force her to rusticate in the country with no chance of ever finding a suitable husband?"

"Honestly, Miss Carlisle, do you truly believe a gentleman of good character will forgive my sister's past as a lady's maid?"

"I do admit, the situation is . . . unusual. However, she stands a better chance at finding a husband here, during the Season, than in the countryside. And hypocritical though it be, her new status as the sister of an earl will do wonders toward erasing anything she may have experienced in the past."

"She is an innocent," he snapped.

Ivy nodded. "Of course."

He closed his eyes briefly and turned his attention back to the hearth.

"We can make this work, my lord. If you take a strong lead, it will lend confidence to your family." Ivy tipped her head to the side with a little smile and tried to catch his eye.

Finally meeting her gaze, the earl nodded once. "I will do this for them. But you should know I intend to explore every possibility of breaking the stipulation that I not return to the sea. I'll show my face in parliament for matters I cannot avoid and see that my mother and Sophia are comfortably settled here. But I'll not remain for the rest of my days living the life of a gentleman of leisure, doing nothing."

"You are most singular, my lord. I do not know any men who

would not jump at this opportunity to live a 'life of leisure.' But whatever legalities you are able to finesse in the future will be your business. Our task now is to ready you to *seem* as though you want to spend your time 'doing nothing.'"

"And you are determined to review this list of yours with me today?"

Ivy nodded. "The sooner, the better."

The earl made no move to rise from his chair but rather studied her face through a slight narrowing of the eyes. "What does this little," he twirled his finger in the air, "arrangement benefit you?"

Ivy thought of Nana with a rueful smile. "My grandmother is most persuasive. And as she and your grandmother were dear friends, I find it an honor to help ease your entrance into Society." Well, perhaps that was stretching the truth a bit. The man was large— commanding—and she found herself flustered more than she'd been . . . ever. To couch her current efforts as an "honor" was, at best, a white lie. What *was* she doing, really? Ivy wasn't certain she understood the whole of it herself.

His eyes seemed to take in every detail as they roamed her face in what she assumed was a quick assessment. He would likely have been a very competent sea captain, had the old earl let him be.

"Tell me, Miss Carlisle," he finally said. "You seem to be all that is good and proper. Excellent bloodlines, no doubt, and land in the family for generations, I would wager. A titled father. Why is it that you are not married yet yourself?"

Ivy tried not to gape at his direct approach. Pinching her lips together, she considered her words very carefully. "There have been . . . circumstances . . . beyond my control. I was to have come out already, but regrettably, it will have to wait." He could dig all he would like—she was not about to air family business to a stranger. Especially the horrifying kind of business that had the Carlisles trying to hold their heads high despite Caroline's indiscretions.

"Got yourself caught kissing someone behind the gazebo, perhaps?" His look was smug, taunting, and she wanted to slap it right off his face.

"Certainly not! And I do not appreciate the insinuation, sir."

He spread his hands wide in a show of innocence. "I insinuate nothing. I merely find myself confused at the fact that someone so clearly suited to wedded bliss seems to have been passed over and disregarded."

Ivy felt her nostrils flare. "I have not been *passed over*. I told you, my Season is yet to come, and I've no doubt I will make a very agreeable match."

"Agreeable to whom? Your family? Parents?"

"All."

"But not necessarily yourself."

"You've been at sea, my lord, and obviously in more ways than one, but surely you realize that love matches are simply an anomaly. They do not happen among the aristocracy, and I do not waste my time imagining otherwise."

"I knew a member of the aristocracy who married for love." The earl's face was calm enough, but he gave away an inner agitation with the subtle lines that tightened around his mouth.

"And it didn't end well, did it?" she murmured. Ivy felt another unwelcome stab of pity for the man. And as unwelcome as it was for her, she knew that pity would be doubly unwelcome for him.

"I suppose I've done little more than prove your point."

"I do wish you could prove me wrong. But I'm afraid you will not." Ivy smiled but felt sad. She was a product of an arranged marriage herself, and she had always known there was very little love lost between her mother and father. Perhaps when she had been a young girl she might have dreamed of marrying her one true, perfect love, but those days were long gone. As much as she wished it otherwise, she knew well enough that the circles in which she moved did not much worry about marital sentiment. As long as both parties were agreeable and practical, a pleasant enough life could be expected.

Seeking to change the topic of conversation, she opened the elegant pocket watch she'd received on her sixteenth birthday from Nana. "But look at the time," she said to the big, sprawling man lounging in the chair opposite her. "We have much to cover today, and I would suggest you go up to your chambers and change into something suitable for a quick jaunt around the park. We can discuss your scheduling while we ride."

Again that flat expression before he rolled his eyes ever so slightly and shook his head. Bracing his hands on the arms of his chair, he had just begun shoving himself upright when she held up a hand.

"One moment, my lord."

He paused, half raised. "Yes?"

"The way you . . . move."

He narrowed his eyes. "What fault could you possibly find with the way I move?"

"It's rather lumbering, almost as one would imagine an elephant, or perhaps a great ape. Gentlemen of the *ton* move with grace, elegance."

Still poised halfway out of the chair, he opened his mouth, then pressed his lips together. He continued to stare at her, and she wondered if he would remain suspended above the seat for an eternity.

One thing was certain—the delicate arms of the Queen Anne chair wouldn't bear it for long.

He bared his teeth at her then in what she assumed he intended to be a smile, and finally stood fully upright. Hands on his hips, he towered over her chair, and she swallowed once, wondering if perhaps she ought to have thought of different animals to use as examples. He didn't seem to have appreciated the comparison.

When he didn't appear inclined to say anything, or perhaps conversation simply eluded him for the moment, Ivy lifted the watch she still held in her hand. Maintaining eye contact with him, she pointed at the watch with one finger.

He shook his head once and left. Ivy decided against calling him back into the room to remind him he really should make a pleasant exit with a light bow and a few polite words before quitting the presence of a lady.

CHAPTER 6

A ride through the park can be quite the most
pleasant part of the day. Always wave cheerfully to
acquaintances and put on an air of happiness.
Mistress Manners' Tips for Every-day Etiquette

The fact that he was riding through Hyde Park in a chauffeured carriage didn't concern Jack so much until he noted several other men who drove their own, smaller carriages. The vehicles were sleek and quick, and he suddenly felt very ridiculous. It was not an emotion he enjoyed. Adding to his sense of frustration was the woman seated next to him, pretty and polished and intending to make a gentleman out of him. And entirely against his will.

"The next time I take a jaunt through this park, I will drive one of these infernal things myself."

Ivy looked at him, her face reflecting her surprise. "Well certainly, you can learn how. Not every gentleman desires such a thing. Many are content with the prestige of merely owning at least two carriages. I'm sure you noticed your four that are currently parked in the mews.

41

And that is just the town home. I suspect the estates in the country will boast more."

Jack frowned, uncomfortable. "I have not earned any of this."

Ivy watched him quietly for a moment, and he wondered what she was thinking. "You are an odd one, my lord," she finally said and turned her attention back to the path that wound its way through the park. "I do not believe I've ever encountered a gentleman who wishes he had earned his wealth. The more helpless the person, the higher his status. If one has the resources to employ an army of servants to do every little thing for the master and lady, he is considered quite well-off indeed." She smiled then, and he could have sworn he saw the slightest twitch of her lips that suggested she found what she said to be folly.

"And what is your opinion on the matter?"

She hesitated. "It hardly signifies what I believe, now, does it? Mine is not to question why."

Jack felt a stab of disappointment. The little lady was conscious of propriety to a fault and would likely never criticize the Society that had produced her. She probably curtseyed in her sleep. "You don't find the mentality of the elite rather ridiculous, Miss Carlisle? A man who cannot be bothered to tie his own cravat or don a suit coat by himself would be laughed off the deck of the *Flying Gull*."

"Be that as it may, traditions are deeply rooted, and I don't foresee them changing anytime soon."

"I'm going to drive my own phaeton," Jack muttered, but he kept the rest of his opinions to himself.

Ivy cast a quick glance in his direction, and he thought he detected a slight shrug. "Of course, my lord."

Jack closed his eyes. "I've told you, I do not wish to be addressed in that manner."

Ivy snapped closed the fan she'd been gently waving, despite the fact that it wasn't a warm morning. "Is it not the custom, sir, for a sailor of higher rank to be addressed by subordinates with a title indicating that lofty sailor's position and setting him apart from the lesser seamen?"

"We are not aboard a ship," he ground out. They rode along in silence for several moments, and Jack observed the people who were taking a turn about the park. Many rode in some sort of conveyance, some walked arm-in-arm. There was much laughter in the air, and cheeks were flushed with excitement. Did people truly have nothing better to do with their time?

"There are some items, some scenarios we must study. I would assume this afternoon is as good as any? And I thought we might stop by and visit your mother and sister. I sent around a calling card this morning and received word back that they would be delighted to have us join them for luncheon."

His mother and Sophia—the two variables in the whole mad scheme that had him worried sick. He knew if they were rebuffed or treated at all badly, his temper would rise to the fore and he would likely ruin everything his grandfather had foisted upon them. For him, it was a nightmare, of course, but for Mary and Sophia—they had practically been lifted out of the gutters and set up in a veritable palace.

He nodded once at Ivy and turned his attention back to the park that rolled by cozily as they traveled the path. He hardly knew the young woman who sat beside him, only that she followed rules and regulations religiously. She might have made a fine sailor, in fact, and the thought had him smiling to himself. The lighter emotion faded quickly as he envisioned Lady Ivy Carlisle shaming his family into submission so that they might present a perfect front for the ridiculous lot that lived in London.

"Miss Carlisle, I would like you to understand very clearly that Sophia and my mother are to be treated with dignity and respect. The fact that they have not had your privileges does not mean they have no worth."

The young woman's brow creased in a frown as she regarded him for some time. "May I tell you again, my lord, that I am the last one in all of England to ever humiliate anyone. I plan to equip your family with the skills necessary to arm themselves against those who might."

"So we have an understanding."

"We do," she said, the slightest hint of bite to her tone. "Not that it was necessary to address again."

"I don't know you, lady. I have been forced into this ridiculous charade completely against my will and seek only after the welfare of my loved ones. You may be a perfectly wonderful person, but my first concern is for them."

"I should hope that it would be, my lord, and before you snap at me again, you may as well accustom yourself to being addressed as your title befits."

"You can address me as 'Jack.'"

"No, I most certainly cannot." Ivy flicked her fan open again and shook her head, focusing her attention on the path before them.

He studied the simple beauty of her profile—the long lashes that framed green eyes, the soft skin, the gently defined jawline that was now quite firmly set. "I am an earl, yes?"

She focused her gaze on him again. "Yes." The tone was wary, as though she knew the question had a catch to it. She was indeed a bright girl.

"Therefore, I command you address me as 'Jack.'"

She flushed. "It is not nearly so simple! In fact, it . . . it . . . it's unseemly!"

Jack sighed. Ivy was clearly genuinely distressed. "We shall make a compromise, then. When we are in the company of others, you may address me as Your Majesty, for all I care. But when we are alone, you will use my given name."

There was a sparkle in her eyes then, and her lips twitched. "Your given name is not 'Jack.'"

Drat. He had become a victim of his own trap. "Please, dear lady, do not call me 'John.' Nobody in my life has ever called me by that name. Not even my own mother."

"And I see yet another flaw in your demand," she said. "We will never be alone."

He couldn't help but grin. "We are alone now."

"We are not alone! We are in a park full of people."

"None of whom are paying attention to a word we say. Not even him." He gestured forward to the driver who sat in front of them, maneuvering the horses. "And you are to be my tutor, my mentor in the art of decent behavior, yes? That will require a certain amount of time, as you yourself have voiced on more than one occasion. So you must call me 'Jack,' or I will tell your grandmother that I will never again allow you entrance into my home."

To her credit, Ivy didn't stammer or beg that he reconsider. Instead, she shot him a flat look that spoke volumes. "You will not do such a thing, and you well know it."

"How little you know me, Miss Carlisle."

She sniffed. "I know enough. And you, sir, I know that you ought to be addressing me as 'Lady Ivy' rather than 'Miss Carlisle.'"

He smiled and held her gaze with his own until she turned away and looked forward again, her papers clutched firmly in her gloved hands. Good—he had distracted her from that infernal List of Torturous Activities for the New Earl of Stansworth.

She really was a pretty young woman. Perhaps the time spent with her might prove diverting after all. He supposed he should be grateful that his spiteful old grandfather hadn't insisted Jack take lessons from some staid valet. A man could certainly do worse than spend his time in the company of a beautiful woman. And when it was finished, he would buy himself a new merchant vessel and leave London and her ridiculous Society far behind.

CHAPTER 7

A lady's home is her sanctuary. It is a haven
for herself and her loved ones.

Mistress Manners' Tips for Every-day Etiquette

I vy stood next to the earl at the door of his mother's new home. It was situated in a quiet corner of a lovely square; flowers in abundance were placed near the gate and the stairs, and the home itself was stately and neat as a pin. It was the very image of domestic bliss, beautifully suited for the mother of a new earl, and Ivy wondered how the inhabitants fared. It caught her by surprise that she felt a modicum of apprehension at meeting Mrs. Elliot and her daughter.

The earl knocked, and the door was answered promptly by a very dignified butler who must have recognized Mr. Elliot—Jack, for heaven's sake, as if she could ever really address him that way—because the man bowed low and ushered them inside. He showed them to a parlor and told them he would alert Mrs. and Miss Elliot to their arrival.

"Was this home part of your grandfather's holdings?" Ivy asked him.

Mr. Elliot looked at her in what she could only define as disgust. "I haven't the least idea," he told her flatly. "For all I know, he pulled it out of thin air."

"Well, you must admit it is lovely." Ivy sat in a delicate chair that afforded a picturesque view of the small front yard. "Ultimately you must be pleased to see them so well housed."

Mr. Elliot wandered to her side and looked out the window. "It is the only part of this arrangement I find to my liking."

She studied him for a moment, appreciating the fine cut of his clothing—a temporary set from another gentleman's canceled order—until his own were available from Mr. Pearson. He looked very smart indeed. It was probably the first time she had really examined him as a man and not with an analytical eye bent on determining a curriculum for a student. Once his grasp of social customs was up to snuff and his accent smoothed over, he would have no problem at all finding himself a suitable bride. As for his claims to return to the sea, well, that was hardly her concern. She frowned a bit at the thought. He was certainly very odd.

"Jack!"

The voice from the doorway drew her attention, and Ivy gazed her first upon the earl's mother. She was tall but frail. Although Jack's appearance clearly mirrored his father's side of the family, Ivy noted he possessed his mother's eyes. They were the same warm golden brown. She was a lovely woman, and Ivy felt a moment of frustration at the old earl who had thrown his son and young bride out of his home and life. Rarely did aristocracy ever marry the lower classes, but it had happened. Mary Elliot's adult life should have been entirely different. Ivy should know Mrs. Elliot from spending time with her at tea. More to the point, the woman should have been titled.

"You look beautiful, Mama." Jack stepped back and held her at arm's length. "The home and the clothing—they suit you well. You are comfortable, then?"

Mrs. Elliot nodded with a light smile and ducked her head a bit, smoothing her hand over perfectly coiffed hair. "It was good of you to call on us last night—we slept well despite the rather quick upheaval. I feel like a girl playing dress-up." Her face was flushed. "This, all of this, it really isn't me."

"It is you." Jack kissed one of her hands and then placed it between both of his. "This is very much overdue."

Ivy, who had stood when the woman entered, now moved forward slightly. Jack must have remembered she was in the room; he cleared his throat and gestured toward her. "Mother, this is Lady Ivy Carlisle. Lady Ivy, my mother, Mrs. Mary Elliot."

Ivy raised a brow at the smooth introduction even as she smiled at the older woman and moved forward to curtsey. Perhaps Jack wasn't as socially inept as he seemed. "Mrs. Elliot, it is such a pleasure to make your acquaintance."

"And yours as well," Mary said, her tone quiet as she curtseyed in return; her gaze connected fleetingly with Ivy's and then shot downward.

Ivy maintained her smile as she waited for Mrs. Elliot to suggest they be seated. The poor woman seemed afraid of her own shadow—the *ton* would eat her alive. Ivy suddenly understood her son's desire to hide her away at the country estate.

The new earl finally motioned to the seating area, and the three attempted to make themselves comfortable as an awkward silence descended upon the room.

This will not do at all. Ivy realized belatedly that it would have been infinitely easier to meet the woman without Jack's heavy-handed presence. She could feel his gaze upon her as though daring her to say the wrong thing to the mother he clearly adored.

For pity's sake.

Ivy made a decision. "Lord Stansworth, I wonder if you would be so kind as to see to some refreshments for your mother and me? I find I am most parched."

He glanced at the bellpull and then back at Ivy, brows drawn. She tipped her head slightly toward the door and silently willed him to get up and leave the room. He looked at her for a moment, and she imagined all sorts of things he was probably saying to her in his head, but he finally stood and sketched a quick bow to them both. "I shall return with some tea then, perhaps? If that would be to your liking, Lady Ivy?"

She offered him a bright smile that she hoped rather perversely would grate on his nerves. "Splendid, my lord."

When she was alone with Mary Elliot, she sighed a bit in relief. "Your son, my lady, is very pleasant and a wonderful conversationalist," she said, wondering if she would be struck dead at the lie, "but I do find that gentlemen have a way of pulling the air right out of a room sometimes, don't you?"

Mary smiled and emitted the slightest of laughs. "I confess, I haven't spent much time in the company of gentlemen. Only my late husband, and that has been . . . well, a very long time."

Ivy nodded. "Mrs. Elliot, if I may speak frankly?"

"Please."

Ivy paused for a moment, choosing her words carefully. She finally decided to be honest. "I can only imagine how odd these circumstances are for you. I do not know how much your son has explained, but my grandmother promised your late father-in-law that I would help ease the new earl's way into Society. I could hardly do so without also seeing to your welfare. My aim is to prepare you for upcoming social events—to perhaps help you know what you might expect."

"We already know what to expect." The voice came from the doorway, and Ivy turned to see a stunning young woman whose features were very near perfection. Ivy credited the fact that she didn't gape at the beauty to her own good upbringing and polish.

Ivy stood. "Miss Sophia Elliot?"

The young woman's lips twitched in a parody of a smile and she entered the room, bobbing a quick curtsey, which Ivy returned. Suddenly everything made sense. Sophia Elliot had not had success as a lady's maid for more than a few months at any one post because she drew too much male attention. A thousand thoughts flew through Ivy's mind as she took in the beautifully full head of dark blonde hair and the same beautiful golden eyes her mother and brother possessed. Sophia Elliot would soon find herself the most eligible young woman on the marriage circuit and the envy of every spiteful girl who would pale in comparison.

"Oh, dear." Ivy's polish gave way to impulse. "We do have a bit of a conundrum. I wonder if you are up to a challenge?"

Sophia cocked a brow. "I would say I'm well versed in the subject of challenge."

"That is a very good thing, then, because if you weren't hated before, you are going to be now."

Sophia blinked.

"And I am your new, very *best,* bosom friend. Miss Elliot, we must suit up and prepare for battle. You know what to expect, you say?" Ivy linked arms with the stunned young woman, who had entered the room clearly prepared to butt heads with Ivy. "I would suggest it will be twice as heinous as you imagined. And here I thought the challenge would be your brother. My dear," she said as she nudged Sophia down on the settee next to her, "tell me exactly what you hope for your future, because despite the fact that you are officially in mourning, I predict that within a month, all of London will be at your feet."

CHAPTER 8

Great care should be taken when partaking of refreshments socially to be cognizant of good manners. Small sips are most appropriate.

Mistress Manners' Tips for Every-day Etiquette

Ivy tapped the end of her pencil against the sheaf of papers she held as she followed one very angry earl from the withdrawing room to the library after returning to his town home. Mercy, but he had long legs, and she was nearly trotting to keep up. Perhaps it had not been a good suggestion that he think of some tokens he might offer should anyone ask him about his grandfather at the funeral.

"No. Absolutely not. I will not say anything in public about that man, especially something that would be considered even remotely positive!" Jack growled over his shoulder as he made his way to the sideboard and uncorked a bottle of port, which he sniffed and then rolled his eyes. "Where is the rum?"

"I am not asking you to deliver the eulogy; the vicar will do that," Ivy said, trying to reason with him. She glanced down at the papers and placed a check mark next to several items she knew Nana had already arranged. "If you would simply thank those in attendance and express your—"

"My *what?* My profound grief? My absolute dismay that he didn't live longer so that we might spend time together before he traveled on to his reserved spot in hell?" Jack lifted the bottle and took a healthy swig of the drink.

Ivy's mouth dropped open, and she closed it with effort. "My lord, surely you see the glasses neatly placed right in front of you?" She waved her pencil at the port glasses in question.

Jack wiped his mouth with the back of his hand and thumped the bottle back onto the sideboard, sloshing a wave of port onto his white sleeve, as he had slung his suit coat over the front hall banister upon entering the house. Ivy briefly closed her eyes.

"I hated the man," Jack said evenly, "and am glad that he's dead. I'll be gladder still when his old bones are shoveled six feet into the ground where the worms will feast and probably die from ingesting the poison that housed his soul."

Ivy blinked. She finally nodded and crossed another item off her list. "I don't suppose we really need you to say anything at all. Perhaps Nana might offer a few thankful sentiments." She cleared her throat and met his gaze, which bore directly into hers. His agitation was evident in his stance—with one hand on his hip and the other still gripping the neck of the bottle, he appeared as one might when preparing to jump into a brawl. His nostrils flared slightly, and the color in his face was elevated.

Mercy, but he was so very agitated. Seeking to goad him into a lighter sense of mind, she pointed to the bottle of port, an object for which she was beginning to feel extreme pity despite its inanimate nature. "You might loosen your hold there," she said. "The glass will withstand only so much pressure before shattering, and then you'll find yourself with a nasty cut. We need you whole and unmarred for shaking hands at the funeral." She meant the last as a jest, and she delivered it with a smile that he did not return. If anything, she imagined she saw him go redder in the face. He lifted the bottle back up and took another long swig.

"Lady Ivy," he said evenly, his voice pitched low, "you do not know me well, and for that reason I will excuse your provocations. If you were a sailor, I would thrash you to within an inch of your life." The gritty accent to his words gave a deeper impression of a man who had most certainly not been raised in London's drawing rooms.

"Hardly the sort of thing one ought to say to a lady," Ivy muttered, trying for a nonchalance she didn't necessarily feel. The man was large and most frighteningly angry; her heart beat a quick staccato and she congratulated herself for standing her ground. Gentlemen of her acquaintance did not get *angry* so much as annoyed. Mildly perturbed. She had overheard Lord Brandswell lose his temper while playing whist at Lady Umpton's ball last Season, but it had passed quickly as his friends had ushered him from the home before he could do any real damage to his reputation as a usually very even-tempered fellow.

"What did you say?"

Ivy swallowed. Where was the man who had attempted charm on their ride through Hyde Park? With a frown, she put her pencil to the paper and made herself a note: *Highly mercurial. Must take care when discussing the late earl.*

"Truly, Lady Ivy, you ought to repeat yourself—if you're going to say something, commit to it!"

Ivy felt her own temper flare, and she wondered fleetingly if the man would eventually drive her to make a scene of her own. She tamped down an irrational urge to shout at him and took a cleansing breath. "Lord Stansworth, you are behaving like a child," she said quietly and moved closer to him. "Pull yourself together! For the love of heaven, you do not have to speak at the man's funeral—in fact, I'll repeat my earlier sentiment that it would be best if you not open your mouth at all. I merely thought to jest with you a bit, but I can see that you are utterly incapable of appreciating any kind of witty or sophisticated humor. I'll not make the mistake again."

The new earl stared at her openly for a moment, his hand still tightly gripping the bottle of port. He had just opened his mouth to reply when the butler appeared at the doorway and cleared his throat.

"My lord, your cousin Mr. Percival Elliot and his wife are here to see you. I have shown them to the drawing room."

Jack transferred his bewildered anger from Ivy to Watkins, the butler, who, to his credit, did not flinch or move a muscle. Years of service in the home of an earl had done the man well.

"I will not receive that man in this house."

Ivy stifled a sigh. "His Lordship will receive his relations in a few minutes," Ivy told Watkins.

"Very good, my lady." Watkins bowed and left.

"What?" Jack stormed after the butler, who wisely did not return to the room. The angry earl stomped over to the door and yelled down the hallway, "Lady Ivy does not live here! Nor does she pay your salary!"

"Mercy," Ivy muttered. She was utterly failing in her duties, and now all of the servants around London would know the new earl was certifiably insane. Nana would not be impressed.

"Lord Stansworth!" She hissed it loudly, and thankfully, the man turned around. His expression was thunderous, and she was fairly certain she saw a vein pulsing in his temple. "Now then," she said. "Go upstairs to your rooms, have Pug help you into a clean shirt, and meet your cousin and his wife." She held up her pencil as he drew in a breath to deliver what she assumed would have been a blast worthy of Admiral Nelson's cannons. "Do bear in mind that this is the man who was the heir to this estate but a week ago. You would be well advised to assess his current inclinations. Discover whether or not he bears you any ill will."

"I do not care if he bears me ill will," Jack raged. "There is one man on this earth I hate second only to my dead grandfather, and it is my father's *cousin!*"

Ivy took a deep breath. "My lord, we have only just returned from a very lovely home that now provides a most suitable residence for your mother and Sophia. I should think perhaps if you keep that uppermost in your mind, you might find saying a few polite words to your cousin a bit more palatable." He was going to have to overcome his irrational hatred of the upper class if he hoped to successfully launch his family into their new life.

Jack closed his eyes and rubbed a hand along the back of his neck. She'd seen him do it before—usually when he was under duress.

"It is not so awful," she murmured, stepping closer to him. "You can manage this—all of this—for their sake."

He didn't respond; his eyes were still closed as he massaged his neck. Silently making his way back to the sideboard, he released his grip on the poor mistreated port bottle and stepped around Ivy.

As he approached the door, she said, "And later, we will discuss effective and proper ways to apologize to a lady for boorish behavior." Why could she not resist goading him? She had no idea. Perhaps some secret part of her heart, the playful part that she habitually shoved into submission, had been fascinated watching him transform from a man to a stampeding bull.

He turned at the door and shot her that flat expression that was becoming familiar. "I have no time for apologies. I have a cousin to entertain."

"Not yet." She twirled her pencil tip at the ceiling. "Go upstairs and change your shirt. You have port all over your sleeve. Of course," she amended, "you could always don the suit coat you threw off the moment we walked in the door. Had you kept it on, that little mishap with the drink wouldn't be nearly so noticeable right now. Many consider it bad form indeed to remove the suit coat during the day, and especially in the presence of a lady."

"You do not seem to realize that the ice on which you tread, Lady Ivy, is very, very thin."

"Then I suppose it is a good thing I skate well," she said brightly and brushed past him, pausing just in the hallway. "No, best to change the shirt," she said and touched a fingertip to his cuff. "This will protrude from the coat." She frowned. "You were serious, I suppose, when you designated Pug as your valet? We may need to track him down. I saw him arguing heatedly with Millie when we arrived— I believe they were headed for the kitchen. Never mind," she said, waving a hand at him and making a decision. "I'll wait outside your dressing room. Should you need help with your cravat, I can assist. Nana taught me how; she insists it is a skill a lady ought to have."

Ivy turned and motioned with her head. "It's just as well," she added when he finally joined her on the stairs, looking for all the world as though he'd taken up residence in a foreign land where he didn't understand the natives, "to keep them waiting just a few minutes. To my knowledge, your cousin did not send a calling card in advance—that is hardly the thing. It is unseemly of him to presume you will see him at a moment's notice."

"Would it not be presumed that one would see family without expecting the same formalities as from the general populace?" Jack said as they climbed the stairs side by side, the bitterness evident in his tone. At least he had recovered his equilibrium enough to resume conversation that didn't involve cursing or sputtering.

"Well, yes," she admitted, "but these are unusual circumstances, are they not? I am probably not mistaken that you've yet to even meet the man." Which was why his extreme hatred of Percival Elliot was all the more baffling to her.

"Would that I should never have to meet the man," he said quietly. His lips thinned and the muscles in his jaw clenched. Ivy felt a softening in her heart for the new earl, who seemed so very unhappy and out of place, so much so that she decided a lesson on The Rules of Climbing Stairs with a Lady could wait.

CHAPTER 9

A visit with relations should be a delightful time to reminisce and create new memories that will be enjoyed for years to come.

Mistress Manners' Tips for Every-day Etiquette

Jack wondered which would happen first—would he disgrace his mother by behaving inappropriately in public or end up in Newgate for murdering Lady Ivy Carlisle? He stood in the dressing room that adjoined his bedroom as she tied his cravat with fingers that were deft and sure. He smelled a subtle scent of something flowery and was angry that he noticed it. The task she performed was oddly intimate, and she was close enough to either strangle or kiss. He didn't imagine there was a man in all of existence who would have blamed him for doing either one.

She was maddening—he was like a fish out of water in his new environment and she insisted on goading him. If he knew for certain that it was intentional, that somehow she meant to tease him, it might be a bit more palatable, but he wondered if she was simply obtuse when it came to communicating with a reluctant pupil. It was true enough that she had admitted to him when they were in the library that she had been jesting, but her timing had been horrid.

Or brilliant.

He couldn't decide which. And now she stood with him, not a foot away, performing the task of a wife or a lover—and she smelled good. It was a welcome distraction from the meeting that awaited him downstairs. Her hair was shiny and curled elegantly in that way ladies did things, and he was tempted to blow softly across her ear in retaliation for making him angry enough to suffer apoplexy.

Say something nice about his grandfather at the funeral? It would be a cold day in Hades before he ever said anything nice about the man. That she would even ask it of him spoke volumes about the fact that she really didn't know him at all. And just when Jack had decided that she might be redeemable—she had charmed his mother and Sophia, after all—she threw out the one suggestion guaranteed to make his blood boil. The fact that his cousin had arrived in the midst of it was only to be expected, he supposed. Better to gather all of the misery he could imagine and stuff it into one afternoon.

"There, now." Ivy patted his cravat. "Perfect." She moved away, regrettably, and retrieved her blasted stack of papers from the side table where she'd plunked them down after putting her pencil behind her ear and making a beeline for his throat when he'd entered the room after changing. She had also tugged on his coat, examined his cuffs, and looked critically at his hair before shrugging a bit.

"Were you a valet in another life, perhaps?" he asked, still feeling surly as he put a finger between his collar and neck. He wondered if she'd tied it so snugly on purpose. "Where did you learn to tie a gentleman's cravat?"

"I told you, Nana insisted. One cannot always be certain a valet will be at the ready—a fact to which we can attest this very mo-ment—so one must know how to make do on one's own."

"Now, there's a novel thought. You told me just this morning that the more helpless one is, the better."

"I didn't say it was something with which I agreed."

"No, you didn't. In fact, you refused to offer an opinion on it at all."

The lady sighed and folded her arms over her papers, which she held to her chest, more the pity. "My lord, I have come to the conclu-sion that very little will be served by being either evasive or diplomatic with you. I suppose it can be attributed to your time on the high seas and away from civilization."

He narrowed his eyes. "What can be attributed to it?"

"Your utter lack of appreciation for societal customs and tradi-tions. A woman is to offer her opinion on only the rarest of occasions, and a gentleman is considered cream of the crop if he has land and an army of servants to see to his every whim."

She turned to leave the room, and he grabbed her arm. "Tell me you don't find that utterly ridiculous," he demanded, his temper still broiling dangerously below the surface.

"Well, of course I do. My mind is full of ideas that I shall probably never share with anyone." Something passed across her face so quickly that Jack figured he must have imagined it. Just a flicker, really, of sadness, perhaps. Or resignation.

"There are places in the world where you could share your ideas freely and not be considered improper," he told her gruffly as he released her arm. He patted it awkwardly, wondering if he should apologize for manhandling her. The women with whom he was accustomed to spending time didn't seem to mind, but he was certain that with this one, he had just broken at least a dozen rules.

She smiled at him rather as one would respond to a child. "I am certain there are such wonderful places."

He raised his eyebrows as she turned and made her way to the door. He followed her, wondering if the pounding in the back of his head would render him useless by nightfall. "You believe I tell stories? I will have you know that sailors are every bit as intelligent as your Society gentlemen, probably more so."

"Says the man who drinks directly from the bottle." She had reached the landing by the time he caught up with her, and she checked her pocket watch as they began descending the stairs. "This is just enough time to have kept them waiting," she said as he searched for something scathing to say. The most he could manage involved several words even he knew were unfit for anywhere but the deck of a ship.

He clamped his jaw shut tightly until they reached the door of the drawing room. He had absolutely no interest in meeting the man on the other side of it, and he tried to imagine his mother and Sophia being ejected from their new home to force himself to see it through.

"You look splendid." Lady Ivy patted his shoulder. "You needn't stay in there overly long—it is merely a quick social call. You probably ought to ring for tea, but you might be forgiven for omitting it, as this is a trying time, what with the family being in mourning."

He opened his eyes wide and stared at his unwanted governess. "Oh, no. You're going in there with me."

Her answering expression was priceless, and he wished he were in a better frame of mind to enjoy it. "But I'm not dressed for it!" she protested.

"You look splendid." He echoed her words. "And if you do not come in here with me, I'm going back upstairs. They can sit in here until they rot."

"Lord Stansworth!" she hissed. She glanced over his shoulder and straightened a bit as Watkins approached. It must have been quite a conundrum for her—cause a scene in front of a servant or go along with his demand? Because he wasn't backing down, and she seemed to know it.

"Why?" she whispered, her features tight.

"Because without a buffer, I will probably kill him."

She lowered her voice and moved closer to him. "My lord, you have absolutely no reason to hate your cousin. You've never even met the man!"

"Lady Ivy, this is a person who never once lifted a finger to help my family, even knowing full well that my father—his cousin—was dead and we were all but starving. My mother attempted once to approach him and he told her that if she would agree to a special 'arrangement' between the two of them, he would provide her with food and lodging for our family."

There. He'd said it, and he felt fresh fury and humiliation for his mother's sake. At the time he'd been too young to fully understand the insult. To say that it made him livid now was a gross understatement.

Comprehension dawned on her face, and she briefly closed her eyes before nodding once. She smoothed a hand across her bodice and lightly blew out a puff of air.

"Do you think you can manage the distress of meeting a member of Society while wearing the wrong dress?" He couldn't help the insult—the lady was without an inkling as to how the rest of the world lived. She and the man in the drawing room were living examples

64

of the Society he loathed, and in which he now found himself embroiled. If he was going to suffer, then so was she.

She shot him a look of reproach, and he caught a smoldering behind her eyes that gave him a grim sense of satisfaction. Perfect. The lady had a temper of her own—that she would now be forced to entertain against her will was only fair. To his amazement, she took a breath and, with a long blink, smoothed her features into a pleasant mask of societal perfection.

"I outrank both your cousin and his wife, so you will introduce me first. As I am a daughter, I am to be presented as 'Lady Ivy Carlisle,' not merely 'Lady Carlisle.' We needn't remain long; if it's any consolation, I would assume they don't wish it either." She paused and looked at him for a moment. "Despite what you might believe of me, or the way I live my life, I am very sorry to hear that your mother was treated so disgustingly. It is inexcusable."

The lady gave a nod to Watkins, who moved around them to the door, which he opened and then announced the Earl of Stansworth and Lady Ivy Carlisle to the couple waiting within.

CHAPTER 10

*Friendships are often to be found in unexpected places
and should be cherished and nurtured.*

Mistress Manners' Tips for Every-day Etiquette

Ivy had seen Percival Elliot and his wife, Clista, on very few occasions and was glad they had not been more frequent. To say that the pair were condescending would have been grossly understating the matter. He was aging well—his muscle had yet to run to fat, and he likely still spent time rowing and playing cricket—and she was a pretty if somewhat cold-looking woman whose tasteful cosmetics were fine from a distance, but rather obvious up close.

Perhaps it was because Jack had told Ivy about his cousin's reprehensible behavior, but as they all sat together in the drawing room, she was hard-pressed to concentrate on what the man was saying. Mary Elliot was all things lovely and kind. How on earth could Percival have attempted to exploit and degrade her when she had gone to him destitute and begging for help?

Ivy cast a sidelong glance at Jack, who sat ramrod straight in a chair that looked ridiculously small underneath him. Ivy sat next to him, and the relatives were together on a settee just opposite them on the other side of a small table. It was a stilted and awkward tableau; undercurrents of discomfort floated so completely around the room she began to think they were palpable.

After the initial introductions and a few protracted moments of uncomfortable silence, Ivy relied on several years' worth of experience at meaningless conversation to break the proverbial ice. "I understand you attended Lord Wilston's charity ball last month?" she said to Clista, who was visibly irritated.

Clista turned her focus from her study of the new earl's face and gave Ivy the benefit of her full attention. "Indeed." She managed a smile. "One can never be too charitable."

"So what do you want?" Jack said, and Ivy restrained the impulse to backhand his shoulder.

Percival and Clista blinked at him in stunned silence before Clista narrowed her eyes slightly and curved up the corner of her mouth in a simulation of what one might call a smile.

Wonderful. You've just made my task a hundred times harder, my lord. Clista had found a chink in Jack's armor—his defensiveness and lack of polish, not to mention his rough accent—and would exploit it to the hilt.

Percival cleared his throat and managed a laugh. "Direct, aren't you, my boy? Well now, we merely thought to see that you're settling into the new house comfortably. Welcome you to the fold, if you will."

Jack watched the man silently for so long that Ivy figured he meant to dismiss the comment altogether. He finally managed a tight smile of his own. "I am very comfortable, thank you."

Percival nodded. "And you have had opportunity to meet your peers in the House of Lords? Many of them are regulars at White's, of course, even when parliament isn't in session."

"I've not had the pleasure of social entertainments," Jack said evenly. "I am in mourning; it's to be expected that I would be preparing for my grandfather's funeral tomorrow."

Ivy bit back a smile at Percival's quick nod and subtly tightened expression. The fact that the old earl had been Jack's grandfather and only Percival's uncle was a trump card heavily in Jack's favor. If Jack could continue to deliver veiled barbs rather than oafish outbursts, there might be hope for him yet.

"And what is your connection to the earl, Lady Ivy?" Clista asked. "Do you spend much of your time here in his home?"

"Our grandmothers were the *dearest* of friends, and the dowager countess and I visit here together and also have called on his Lordship's mother and sister during this time of loss."

"Oh, Lady Carlisle is here now? I should love to see her." Clista had a glint in her eye that Ivy didn't particularly appreciate.

"Regrettably, she tires so easily these days that she is currently resting in one of his Lordship's upstairs rooms."

"Yes, regrettably."

Jack shifted in his chair, and Ivy thought she might have heard a growl.

"Had his Lordship received advance notice of your visit, he would have been more fully prepared to entertain you," Ivy said, creasing her brow, "but the staff is consumed with preparing for the late earl's funeral, you understand."

"We do understand indeed." Clista gave a nod and a sympathetic frown of her own. "*We* are family, after all."

"Of course." Ivy resisted balling her hands into fists, but only just. She kept them demurely in her lap, one resting gently atop the other.

Clista turned her attention to Jack. "Cousin, should you have need of anything at all, please know we are at your complete disposal." She placed her hand on her chest. "This is such a trying time for all of us."

"I imagine it is," Jack said.

"And your dear mother and sister—please do have them call on me soon."

"Not likely."

"They are also avoiding Society as yet," Ivy said. "It would hardly be appropriate, of course, to be making social calls so soon after the death of Mrs. Elliot's father-in-law."

Percival cleared his throat and shifted forward on the seat. "Well then, John, when the funeral has concluded and you are ready to go about town, I would be happy to show you the lie of the land, so to speak," he said with a wink.

Jack stood. "I will contact you, should I have need."

Ivy also stood, as did Jack's cousins. Considering the way he had treated Mary, Percival was fortunate that Jack hadn't planted his fist right in the man's face upon entering the room. As it was, Ivy felt absurdly proud of the new earl's restraint. With bows and curtseys all around, the Elliots took their leave.

"All things considered, well done, my lord." Ivy grimaced at the door. "But if Percival Elliot outlives you, he is next in line again to inherit, yes?"

"Unfortunately," Jack grumbled. "And after him, my mother says it's his son, 'little Percy.' Unless I produce an heir."

"Might I suggest you remain watchful?"

Jack raised a brow. "You think he would orchestrate my demise?"

"I do not know that, precisely, but I wouldn't put anything past *her*. I do believe she wants this house and all that goes with it. "

Jack stood in the small, enclosed garden at the back of the house and stared into the distance at nothing in particular. His gut still churned uncomfortably in the aftermath of the visit with his father's cousin and the man's equally odious wife. He felt trapped and angry, and neither was a circumstance for which he had ever had any tolerance.

Lady Ivy, to her credit, had saved the visit with his relatives, neatly dodging Clista's barbs and managing to keep the whole affair, if not actually comfortable, at least bearable. He sincerely hoped he would have to endure such unpleasantness only on the rarest of occasions in the future, and he would move heaven and earth, if necessary, to keep his mother out of Percival's clutches. Several years had passed, it was true, but Mary Elliot was still a beautiful woman, and unless Jack had suddenly become inept at reading people, Percival was still a lecher. He had leered at Lady Ivy one too many times for Jack's liking.

He heard the door open behind him and sensed Ivy's presence without even sparing her a glance as she joined him in the garden. "I thought you were leaving," he said, his eye still fixed on the sky beyond the wall.

"I was. I returned."

He finally glanced at her. "Did you forget something?"

"I want you to know that I . . . that I . . ." She chewed on her lip for a moment, her arms holding her papers across her chest. "I should hate for you to think for even a moment that I condone Percival Elliot's behavior toward your mother."

"You said as much earlier. I heard it."

"Did you?" Her gaze was frank, unblinking. She flushed a bit but forged ahead. "I believe you have an opinion of me that is fixed quite firmly. I do not find all members of fine Society to be above reproach, or even likable. My entire effort—" she waved a hand in the air, "with this endeavor is to see your family well placed. That they must seek to be accepted by people of your cousin's ilk—well, it is insulting, to say the least."

He found himself a bit confused. Perhaps there was more depth to the woman than he'd previously thought. She had nothing to gain by sharing such things with him—she had only to do her appointed task and be finished with it. Why did she care for his good opinion?

"Thank you," he said, hearing the stiffness in his tone. He felt as though he should say something else, but he was at a loss.

She finally nodded and turned to leave.

"Just a moment." He reached out and caught her arm. "Thank you for your support today. I . . . I appreciate your good thoughts about my mother and Sophia."

"You're most welcome." She offered a slight smile. "Your mother is genteel, and her behavior will be above reproach, I am certain. And Sophia—I do believe that girl can withstand the most blistering of storms."

"You anticipate a storm, then?" He realized belatedly he still held her arm. He shoved his hands in his pockets.

Ivy frowned. "Unfortunately, yes. But your reactions will help determine whether or not the storm lasts."

Jack looked back out over the garden, his heart sinking even as he thought himself a fool. He had known it would be difficult, but to hear Ivy verbalize it made everything seem somehow more real.

"You are not alone, Jack," Ivy said softly. "You will see—not all of Society is reprehensible, and you have friends."

He laughed without mirth. "I have no friends."

"You have me. It is as good a beginning as any."

Jack turned his attention to her again and noted the gentle smile on her lips.

"And you have your family," she continued. "And my Nana. All we really need in life are a few good friends, yes?"

He nodded against his will and extended his hand, which she took with a smile. "We will make this thing work."

Jack had his misgivings, but he kept them to himself and instead allowed himself the luxury of rubbing his thumb along the back of her hand. She had such soft skin. He noted the look of awareness that crossed her features, and she flushed, pulling her hand back. She wrapped her arms around the papers as though they were her security.

He smiled at her. "What do you have written down on all that? Surely your entire stack of papers isn't filled with lists of things for me to learn how to do."

Ivy took a step back. "No. I have some other things as well."

"Such as?"

"Oh, just some things I wrote." She was now backing her way to the door.

Following her, his curiosity piqued, he raised a brow. "What kind of things?"

"For my Nana." She opened the door leading into the library. "I will see you tomorrow, of course, at the funeral. Then, as soon thereafter as is reasonable, I thought perhaps we might arrange a shopping trip for Sophia and your mother."

The change of topic was entirely too quick, and as a sailor who had grilled more than one man in an effort to ferret out the truth of a matter, he recognized hedging when he saw it. "Why, Lady Ivy, I do believe you are hiding something."

"Nonsense." She lifted her chin a notch. "I have absolutely nothing to hide."

"Then let me see your papers," he said, feeling the smirk on his face.

"I have things to do." Ivy began walking again. "Until tomorrow."

Jack watched her retreating figure and smiled. A new challenge was just the thing his frustrated mind required. One way or another, he would discover what the little lady had hidden on her papers. And anything that would take his mind off of his present circumstances was a welcome distraction.

CHAPTER 11

*When attending a funeral, great care should be taken
to consider the bereaved, and the greatest respect should
be honored them as they lay a loved one to rest.*

Mistress Manners' Tips for Every-day Etiquette

The church in the village near the Stansworth country estate was packed to the rafters with London's best, who came to offer their condolences at the loss one of their own. Jack took in the surroundings with a fair amount of disgust—he would wager his entire inheritance that there wasn't a genuine mourner among them.

Sophia sat next to him, stiff and defensive, and their mother sat on Jack's other side. He reached over and clasped Mary's hand, giving it a reassuring squeeze. Mary looked up at him through the black lace that trimmed the edge of a beautiful black hat that had cost more than the amount Mary had earned in a year in her work as a seamstress. She was uncomfortable—it was evident in the droop of her thin shoulders and the wariness in her eyes.

Cousin Percival and his wife, Clista, were in attendance, along with their ten-year-old son, Little Percy, who set Jack's teeth on edge at first sight. Ivy Carlisle, her grandmother, and her parents occupied the bench behind his, and Jack was oddly grateful for the support. He knew so few people, and trusted even fewer, so for them to have made the effort to attend was a bolster to alleviate Jack's little family's sense of uncertainty.

The vicar began the services, and Jack fought the urge to pull out his pocket watch. If he could make it through the day without being rude to anyone, he would call it a success. The holy man droned on interminably; Jack knew the vicar was long-winded when even Mary began to fidget in her seat.

The service drew to a close, and Jack guided his mother and Sophia down the long aisle behind the coffin as the guests stood to watch them pass. The ridiculousness of the charade struck him for the hundredth time, and he knew full well that he would never have attended had it not been for his mother and sister.

They followed the coffin out to the churchyard, a slow process that seemed not only to drag but to reverse time. Sophia seemed unusually tense, and he turned his attention to her. "How are you faring?" he asked the beautiful young woman who had grown out of childhood so rapidly he must have missed it when he blinked.

Sophia shook her head, her lips pursed. "I saw a few people I know and would rather not know."

His heart sank for her. "Former employers?"

She nodded.

"I can call them out, if you'd like."

Sophia turned to him, her mouth twitching in what was probably a very reluctant smile. "Pistols at dawn are scarcely the thing in our day. But I do appreciate the sentiment."

He was leery of broaching a sensitive subject, but he pushed forward anyway. "Were you . . . that is . . . were you ever forced against your will?"

Sophia's eyes narrowed. "Very nearly, but I managed an escape. The mistress of the house turned me out the same day with no references."

"I am sorry that I was unable to protect you further."

Sophia laid a hand on his arm. "You did everything we needed you to do. You sent money, you stayed with us while in port. You were like a father to me when I had none."

Mary huddled under her umbrella in the drizzling rain, and Jack wondered what she was thinking. She put her handkerchief to her mouth and coughed into it; Jack had witnessed her illness over the last few days. He hoped that with better living conditions, she would improve. But in the meantime, it was undoubtedly time to call in a doctor, and his resolve was confirmed when he glanced at Sophia, who knew their mother better than anyone and was watching Mary with concern clearly stamped on her features.

"What do you think of the country estate?" Jack asked Mary. "I am considering the notion of coming to stay here in the next few weeks—I wonder if you would enjoy some time away from the city?"

His mother looked at him with a smile. "I think I would enjoy that very much."

Jack led his mother and his sister to the burial plot, where a crowd had already begun to gather. He fully realized what a spectacle the whole thing was when he spied a few men who had pens poised and ready to record the moment for their newspapers.

Glancing over his shoulder, he spied Ivy and her grandmother picking their way across the lawn, Ivy holding an umbrella to shelter them. They settled in next to his family and, at a nod from the vicar, Nana stepped forward to express a few sentiments.

She had chosen her words carefully; Jack admitted a certain sense of awe that the woman paid tribute and yet didn't really say anything about the supposed goodness of his late grandfather. He glanced at Ivy, who winked at him with the slightest twitch of a smile upon her lips. How odd that his heart felt a fraction lighter. Finding an ally in the midst of his current chaos proved to be a strength he hadn't known he needed.

At the completion of the graveside ceremony, Jack stared down at the box that held his grandfather, his flesh and blood, and felt the sting of tears that had nothing to do with sorrow over the man's death, but everything to do with the misery the old man had wrought.

"Are you well?" Ivy asked him and he glanced to his side, wondering how long she'd been standing there.

He nodded and blinked, refusing to allow the tears to fall. "He was an awful person," he murmured to Ivy. "Hateful, spiteful, and selfish."

"You can change the tide." She looked up at him through a black veil that didn't disguise the brilliant green of her eyes. "Someday you will have grandchildren whose grief at your burial will be genuine and heartfelt."

Jack shook his head. "I don't care to ever marry."

Ivy's eyes widened fractionally. "If you don't produce an heir, the title will eventually fall to Percival and Clista's son."

Drat. She was right. The reminder of Little Percy at the helm of anything was more than Jack could stomach.

"Not to worry," she murmured and patted his arm. "There are

many eligible young ladies this Season—we shall find you the perfect match."

He thought that Lady Ivy had better find him a wife who wouldn't care that her husband lived on the high seas, then, but he didn't say as much to her. Let her have her delusions if they made her happy. He opened his mouth to reply, but cut himself off at the look on Ivy's face. Her gaze was fixed at a point beyond his shoulder, and he turned to see Sophia and another woman in a conversation that looked innocent enough on the surface, but the set to Sophia's features was one he recognized. Apparently, Lady Ivy understood it as well.

He took a step toward them when he registered Ivy's hand on his arm. "My lord," she said, "please allow me."

They walked together to Sophia and the woman, Jack seething already without even knowing the substance of the conversation. Ivy must have sensed it, because she glanced up at him and tightened her grip. "Not a word," she murmured.

When they reached the women, Ivy dropped her hand from Jack's sleeve and instead threaded her other arm through Sophia's. "We must be going along to the house, Miss Elliot. I hate to cut short your little chat." Ivy looked at the other woman, who by now had craned her neck to see Jack staring down at her.

"Oh, Lady Finster! I didn't recognize you without your daughters in tow," Ivy said to the woman, her words and tone pleasant enough. "But how delightful you've had a chance to meet Miss Elliot, even though it is during this most somber time."

Lady Finster tore her gaze from Jack and looked at Ivy. She straightened her shoulders a bit and returned a tight smile that nobody would ever mistake as genuine. "I have already met Miss

Elliot," the lady said, "when she worked in my home as a maid to my daughters."

Ivy laughed then and leaned forward slightly, as though suggesting something conspiratorial between them. "How amusing, is it not? Life with its twists and turns. Miss Elliot is the sister of an earl!"

Lady Finster narrowed her eyes and leaned forward a bit herself. "Once a maid, always a maid."

Jack shifted his weight, and Ivy must have sensed it because she held her hand up, her fingers lightly brushing his sleeve.

"Lady Finster, rather gauche of me to mention it, of course, but I understand your husband's gambling debts have placed a strain on the household budget. Miss Elliot is most generous and might entertain the notion of offering a job to either Sally or Sarah, should the need arise. How humiliating it would be to see your house and holdings sold off at auction, and for Lord Finster to be clapped in irons. Why, when that happened last season to the Staffords, it was all the *ton* could talk about for simply ages."

Lady Finster's complexion turned an alarming shade of red. "My daughters will not work—and especially not for that trollop," she hissed and pointed at Sophia.

Ivy's eyes narrowed, and for all that Jack's rage was close to boiling over, he sensed hers was far worse. That she controlled it was a sight to behold, and he watched as much in fascination as in anger as Lady Ivy Carlisle put the woman in her place.

"Perhaps, Lady Finster, you ought to keep a tighter rein on your husband. You might not only find your coffers much improved but also your ability to keep a lady's maid for longer than a fortnight before his baser instincts get the better of him."

Lady Finster made a sound of outrage. "That girl seduced my husband!"

Ivy's face lost all sense of pretended charm. "That must be the most absurd thing I have ever heard. Your husband is hideous, madam, and, if nothing else, Miss Elliot does not want ugly children. Good day to you."

Ivy stood straight, her arm still looped with Sophia's. Jack caught a sheen over Sophia's eyes as Ivy turned her away and left the gaping Lady Finster.

"Do not ever speak to my sister again," he said to Lady Finster in a low undertone and then turned and followed Ivy and Sophia out of the churchyard to a waiting carriage.

CHAPTER 12

*One's table manners are indicative of one's
breeding and training—or lack thereof.*

Mistress Manners' Tips for Every-day Etiquette

With the burden of the funeral behind them, Ivy Carlisle had
wasted no time resuming Jack's lessons on becoming a gentleman. Today she motioned for Jack to sit at the head of the dining
table and then stood at his shoulder. "You did spend some time in the
navy, yes? Perhaps you already understand the fundamentals behind
the place setting?"

He looked at her with an eye roll but said nothing.

"Right, then. It really is very simple," she said, hoping it would
indeed prove to be. "All you must remember is to start with the outer
silverware first and work your way in as the courses progress. And the
dessert implements are here, at the top of the plate."

Jack shook his head. "I find it ridiculous that people should care
which fork I use to eat meat."

Ivy waved a hand at him as she made her way to the opposite end of the table. "We have little time for what you might or might not find ridiculous. Now that a decent amount of time has elapsed since the funeral, I made an appointment with Madame Fitzgibbons later in the day for Sophia and Mary to purchase bonnets, ribbons, and handkerchiefs."

"Excellent," he said, his expression brightening fractionally. "You will enjoy that, I'm sure."

Ivy signaled the footman to place the first course of the light luncheon before them. "I'm sure I will. And you shall, as well."

"I am not going to a bonnet fitting," he said as the footman placed a bowl of soup at Ivy's place setting and then one at Jack's.

"But you are." Ivy shot him a smile and hoped he wouldn't dig in his heels. "A gentleman will frequently attend such things with a wife or mother, but the true reason for our outing is that the *ton* might begin seeing you out and about with your mother and sister. They are in mourning still, it's true, but as they hardly knew the earl, we do have a certain degree of latitude. You will continue to wear all black, but then, I don't suppose you would ever choose to wear otherwise, would you? Somehow I don't see you dressing as a dandy."

He shuddered and picked up his spoon. "I must wait to eat until you've taken your first bite, isn't that so?"

She smiled widely. "Why, yes! Excellent, my lord." She carefully took a spoonful of soup, pleased that he knew something of etiquette without her having to drill it into him first. Her optimism took a quick downturn as the slurping sounds from his end of the table invaded her senses.

"You mustn't slurp," she told him, her spoon poised in midair.

"I did not slurp." He looked at Ivy over his own raised spoon.

"You did, my lord. You slurped."

"Allow me to demonstrate the method with which we ate aboard ship on occasion." Jack placed his spoon down and raised the bowl to his lips. Ivy watched in fascinated horror as he drained the whole bowl in a few moments.

Ivy closed her eyes and then opened them, leveling him with a stare. "Why must you be so stubborn?"

"I am not stubborn at all, good lady." Jack smiled and wiped at his mouth with a snowy white linen napkin. "Merely efficient."

"You cannot do that at a dinner, Jack, you will be ousted."

Jack sat back in his seat, and Ivy finally set her spoon down. He stared at her for a long moment, holding her gaze. It had become a battle of wills, Ivy realized, and she finally sighed, allowing him the victory.

"Very well. Perhaps your mother will be able to make more of an impression on you than I have."

His eyelids dropped to half-mast. "You're going to tell my mother that I drank my soup directly from the bowl?"

Ivy sniffed. "I am indeed. She will be most dissatisfied, I would imagine."

Jack's lips twitched. "You know nothing about my mother."

"I know she is genteel and kind. I highly doubt she would tolerate soup slurping or soup *drinking* in any circumstance." Ivy tried to maintain a sense of outrage—of irritation, at the very least—but found herself quite distracted by the new lord, whose shoulders filled his suit coat to perfection and whose dark curls just brushed the tip of his collar. That he watched her with a lazy smirk ought to have set her on edge. Instead, she found herself ogling the man.

"My mother is genteel and kind. You are correct."

"Then you are seeking to goad me." Ivy suddenly felt her face flush.

"It seems only fair. You have certainly made a good showing of goading me over the past weeks."

"Do you know how to eat properly, then? We needn't waste our time." The irritation surfaced, and Ivy was glad for it.

Jack nodded and sat up in his seat. "I do know how to eat."

"Properly."

"Properly." Jack signaled the footman, who cleared their bowls and brought the second course. "We need not practice table manners, but as lunch is ready and waiting, we ought to indulge. We do have some time before your wretched hat-fitting appointment, I would assume?"

Ivy nodded, feeling a sense of relief that he would be able to handle himself during a meal. She wondered if there were other tasks on her list she could cross off, things that he already knew how to do. Short of hiring an elocution tutor, she wasn't certain how to soften his rough accent. His choice of words was always appropriate—intelligent, even—but his delivery was still, at times, very ungentlemanly.

The rest of the meal continued pleasantly enough, with Jack answering her questions in an annoyingly polite manner that Ivy strongly suspected was wholly sarcastic. By the time they finished eating and made their way to the front hall to go out and meet Jack's mother and Sophia at the milliner's, Ivy was relieved to find the pretense at an end. Jack Elliot as a blandly polite gentleman was . . . bland.

But wasn't that her goal? To transform him into a blandly polite gentleman? She chewed on her lip for a moment as Watkins retrieved her pelisse and reticule. With deft hands, Jack took the pelisse and swung it about her shoulders. He gestured to the front door, indicating that she should precede him.

Ivy narrowed her eyes. "Why are you suddenly so solicitous about bonnet shopping?"

"It will do me some good to get outside." The look on his face was affable.

She didn't trust it for a moment, but she exited the house and moved to the waiting carriage. Whatever he had brewing in his head would hopefully be nothing she should worry about. Or nothing she couldn't fix after the fact.

Jack smiled at all the right times and voiced the correct compliments to Madame Fitzgibbons, conscious of the fact that the sooner he mastered all of Lady Ivy's skills, the sooner he would be finished with the whole thing. He had convinced her that his table manners were passable, and she had stopped trying to instruct him. He didn't know why it had taken him so long to realize that if he cooperated, they would be done much more quickly and he could work at finding his way back to the sea.

A lump formed in his throat as he watched his mother and Sophia navigate the shop under the ever-vigilant and helpful eye of Lady Ivy Carlisle. He had to admit a certain amount of gratitude for the young woman. He would never have been able to ease Mary's and Sophia's entrance into Society without the help, and the more he observed, the more he became convinced that Ivy—for all her insistence upon rules and regulations—was very tender at heart.

And she was clever. That she had managed to build a level of trust with Sophia was nothing short of a miracle. Sophia had even confided in him earlier that if anyone other than Lady Ivy had attempted to tell Sophia what she could and could not do, she would have done that person bodily harm and then run for the hills. "She ought to make me very angry," Sophia had told him, "yet she does not."

He did agree with that much. Well, for the most part. He had found himself angry with her on occasion, but there was something about her demeanor that made it impossible to remain that way for long.

The woman in question walked toward him as his mother and Sophia continued perusing bonnets and ribbons with Madame Fitzgibbons. "I think we will have them nicely outfitted within a week or two," Ivy told him when she reached his side, "and they do have enough things for the immediate future. You will all wear black, of course, for some time longer."

"In mourning for that—that—" He wanted to curse a blue streak, but instead rubbed a hand along the back of his neck. "I had forgotten, and I thank you not at all for reminding me."

"It will go quickly, Jack, and be over before you know it."

"I've noticed you address me as 'Jack' only when you are attempting to placate me or convince me to do something."

The corner of her mouth twitched in a smile. "And it has worked thus far, has it not?"

"I shall have to be on guard, I suppose, against your devious feminine wiles."

"Pooh." She waved her hand. "I am utterly transparent and simple."

He laughed then, unable to help himself. He noticed his mother and sister looking at him in some surprise and he wondered if they'd ever seen him laugh. It had probably been a very long time.

He cleared his throat, feeling suddenly rather embarrassed and sheepish. It was sobering to realize his expressions of joy were so few and far between. If nothing else, it served to solidify his determination to see the charade through. For their sake, as Ivy was always suggesting. He would find his own way back to sea when things were settled for Mary and Sophia. And Ivy would look after them when he eventually left. He felt certain of that.

"I do believe they're finished," Ivy said. "And we thank you most heartily for joining us on our shopping adventure. You would now be perfectly within your rights to visit White's for the afternoon."

Jack rolled his eyes as Mary and Sophia gathered wrapped parcels from the shopkeeper's assistant. "I really do not care to visit a gentlemen's club. I have no use for forming associations with people who do nothing but live lives of leisure and spend their time betting on horse racing."

"You might find yourself surprised—White's and Brooks both see their fair share of war veterans. Real men." She winked at him as he opened the door for the three women to exit before him.

"I am doing my utmost to convince your brother to visit White's," Ivy told Sophia, who looked at him with a grin.

"You must, Jack. It is quite the place to see and be seen," Sophia said as Jack moved to the street and opened the carriage door. The footman scrambled down and gathered the women's packages, placing them in the hold at the back of the carriage.

"Really, Soph, I'd rather thought you would be on my side."

"Are we not all on the same side now?" Sophia said as he handed first their mother, then Sophia into the carriage. "The arrogant, wastrel side? No offense to you, Lady Ivy."

Ivy smiled at her. "None taken. And furthermore," she added, turning her attention to Jack as she placed her gloved hand in his, "you must darken the door if for no other reason than to place a few wagers in the betting book. You are a peer now, so you must do your duty and bet on something utterly ridiculous."

"Such as?" He helped her up into the carriage behind Sophia.

"Well, last month Alvanley and a friend made a wager of three thousand pounds over two raindrops on the window—which one would reach the bottom of the windowpane first."

Jack stared at her, slack jawed, and finally managed to close his mouth.

"Get in then, my lord, and we will drop you by White's. You can meet up with us later at home for dinner."

"I do not need to go to White's," Jack muttered as he climbed into the carriage.

"You cannot live the life of a recluse, my lord. There are certain places where it would behoove you to be seen."

"Really, Jack," Sophia added, "one would think you were afraid."

Jack looked sharply at his sister, who widened her eyes in what was most certainly mock innocence.

Mary leaned forward and clasped Jack's hand. "You do not need to do anything against your wishes," she said. "We shall be just fine— Lady Ivy is helping us make a very good impression."

Jack clenched his teeth together and rapped on the carriage roof. When the driver slowed, Jack stuck his head out the window and instructed him to swing by White's.

CHAPTER 13

A beautiful work of art is like a window to the soul of the artist and should be respected as such.

Mistress Manners' Tips for Every-day Etiquette

Ivy held back a smirk as Jack climbed down from the carriage in front of White's Gentlemen's Club. She almost felt sorry for him as the driver pulled away—she looked out the back window to see Jack standing on the pavement in front of the establishment, his expression an odd combination of anger and confusion.

"Oh, dear," Mary said.

"He will do just fine," Ivy told her. "He must make some acquaintances among the men."

Sophia also looked out the back window, a dubious expression crossing her face. "I'm not certain," the young woman said. "He looks a bit lost."

"He must do this on his own. For one thing, I am not allowed to enter White's and introduce him, and for another, he needs to learn to introduce himself. He will be laughed out of town if I am the one continually paving the path for him."

Sophia looked at Ivy, doubt still clear on her features. "He's rather large and has spent the bulk of his life at sea. I don't believe he would be bullied much, even if you were to do all the introductions for him."

"Bullied, no. Cut? Dismissed? Ignored as one of no consequence? Yes. None of which are good for the two of you."

"Would you join us for tea?" Mary blurted out and looked rather surprised at herself.

Ivy smiled. "I would love to, Mrs. Elliot."

The ride to the women's home was uneventful, and the pitter-patter of rain that now fell from the sky was soothing. Upon their arrival, the footman carried the women's parcels to the house, and the housekeeper, Mrs. Hendersen, ushered them all inside and out of the weather.

Ivy waited for Mary to instruct the staff, and when she seemed at a bit of a loss, Ivy glanced at Sophia.

"We will take tea in the parlor," Sophia told the housekeeper as she, Mary, and Ivy removed their outerwear.

"Very good, Miss," Mrs. Hendersen said and took their wet things with her.

Ivy glanced at Mary as she followed the women into the parlor. The poor lady had absolutely no confidence in herself. A lifetime of hard living had taken its toll; Ivy figured hardships made a person either strong and slightly angry, like Sophia, or withdrawn and afraid, like Mary. Mary would fare well as long as she had a housekeeper who wouldn't take advantage of the fact that her mistress was disinclined to give orders, but should Mrs. Hendersen ever leave her post, Mary might not be so lucky with someone else.

Ivy wondered if Sophia's mind was on similar matters as they took seats in the parlor. Mary gathered some embroidery in her lap, and Sophia stared at her mother pensively. "You are the mistress of the house now, Mama." Sophia's tone was soft. "It is yours to control."

Mary glanced up with a flush and then looked down at her embroidery again. "I do not know how," she murmured.

Ivy pursed her lips and studied the woman, thinking. There had to be a way of teaching her how to be the lady of the house. How odd it was to see that someone struggled with the very thing Ivy had been raised to do. Ivy's own mother ran a tight household, and Ivy had always taken it for granted that someday she would as well.

She would have to find a way to build Mary's confidence, but, in the meantime, perhaps the woman could merely play the part. "Mrs. Elliot," Ivy said, "did you ever play pretend as a child?"

Mary looked at her, brows drawn in confusion. "Yes, I suppose I did. There wasn't much time to play, but when we did, my sister and I pretended we were princesses in a castle."

"Perfect." Ivy nodded. "What we are going to do this week is play pretend. You are the lady of the house, and, as such, are in control of the servants, the house, and everything in it. You are going to act as if this is the most natural thing in the world to you. You will play the part of mistress of the home, and you will feel infinitely better."

Mary nodded slightly. "I suppose, it's just . . ." Mary cleared her throat, and Ivy felt her own clog up a bit. "I do not know how, Lady Ivy. I am a fraud in this place."

Ivy leaned toward Mary. "You are not a fraud. You should have been living this role from the moment you married your husband. You were temporarily displaced, and now the fates have intervened to make things right. You must allow yourself to believe this, and if you find that you cannot, simply pretend you do. Before you know it, you will no longer be pretending."

Mary tilted her head to the side and observed Ivy with what she could only define as hope. Ivy nodded at the woman. "You can do this, Mrs. Elliot."

Ivy glanced at Sophia, who studied her carefully. Sophia finally gave her a slight nod, and Ivy felt absurdly pleased at the young woman's approval.

Turning back to Mary, Ivy looked at the embroidery piece Mary held in her hands. "That is a work of art," Ivy told her. "You are amazingly talented."

"She also paints," Sophia said.

"Sophia, really." Mary ducked her head again.

"I brought them from the closet at our other house. Here's one, in fact, that I'm going to put over the mantle." Sophia stood and retrieved a canvas that had been stashed behind a small desk against the wall.

Sophia turned the painting around, and Ivy sucked in a breath. The work was done in oils and depicted a mother and child seated in a garden. "Oh, Mrs. Elliot," Ivy said, collecting her wits, "this is exquisite!"

Mary blushed but offered the ghost of a smile. "It's just something I've always dabbled in. Sophia, I cannot believe you brought them with us."

Sophia looked at Mary, her expression hard. "Painting is the one thing that keeps you sane, Mama. And Lady Ivy is right—it is exquisite."

Ivy stood and made her way to the mantle. Without first asking permission, she removed the rather bland painting of fruit in a bowl and motioned to Sophia. Taking one side of the canvas, with Sophia holding the other, they placed Mary's piece on the wall.

Ivy felt her eyes sting as she and Sophia moved back to examine the art. "We must find a suitable frame. And I must see the others, Sophia. Nana hosts an art show each year, and this one, at least, must go on display."

"I could never!" Mary's voice was the most firm Ivy had ever heard it.

"Yes, you can," Sophia shot back. Taking a deep breath, Sophia softened her features and regarded her mother. "Mama. Finally, a place for others to see what you create."

"You wouldn't have to attend the showing if you'd rather not," Ivy told her, glancing at the older woman's tense face. "There are plenty of artists who would rather remain anonymous. But please do say you'll give me permission to put your work on display. Such talent should not be hidden under a bushel."

"And Mama," Sophia said, her eyes alight as though an idea had only just occurred to her, "now that you have time at your disposal, you can paint all you'd like! We'll transform one of the rooms upstairs into a studio for you."

Mary looked from Ivy to Sophia and back again. "It would be rather lovely," Mary admitted. "I never even considered the possibility. It's as though I am still wandering through a dream."

"You will never again have to return to your former life," Ivy told the woman. She looked at the piece on the wall and placed a hand lightly to her chest. "Absolutely stunning," she murmured.

"Quite," Sophia agreed.

Jack sat in a comfortable armchair at White's and looked around. The famed Beau Brummell held court by the front window, looking polished and pressed as ever. Jack had heard of the dandy; Brummell was the Prince Regent's bosom friend, and the others who currently flocked to his side looked at the man as though the sun rose and set in his face.

Obsequious, the lot of them. There was no hope for it; Jack would never find himself comfortable in a gentlemen's club—little Miss Carlisle was going to have to find another way for him to represent his family well. He doubted very much he would be able to stomach more than an hour in the company of the social elite.

Another man whose boredom seemed to rival Jack's made his way to an empty chair in the seating area Jack had claimed and motioned to it with a brow raised in question.

"Be my guest," Jack said.

The other man offered his hand. "Anthony Blake," he said. "And you would be the new Earl of Stansworth? Your name is all over the betting book."

Mr. Blake sprawled comfortably in the chair.

"Jack Elliot," Jack said with a nod.

"My condolences on the earldom," Anthony said. "I'm the second son—comfortably the spare until my brother up and died."

Jack raised a brow at the man, who was easily as broad through the shoulders as Jack. He had black hair, dark eyes, and tanned skin, as though he had recently spent time in the tropics. "You were called home, then?"

Anthony Blake nodded, studying Jack. "Very astute observation.

Had a commission in the military," he said. "Would much rather have stayed in Spain than return home to the drizzle."

Jack nodded. "I was set to command my own ship."

"Again, my condolences."

"I hope to return to sea before long."

Anthony raised a brow. "You are an optimistic one, aren't you. Trust me, good man, once you're sucked into the peerage, there's no getting out."

Jack ran a hand through his hair. "Well, this is unacceptable. I am not going to waste my time in this place, day after day. I'll be a candidate for bedlam."

"Agreed. But it's either this or joining the neighbors for afternoon tea."

Jack felt stifled. It was as though the room was closing in on him, the walls moving ever closer, threatening to crush him as he sat in a chair, living a life of luxury. "There must be more to it," he muttered.

He finally looked over at his companion, who was watching him intently.

"You have country estates," Anthony said. "If it's anything like my family's land, there is work to be done. I won't be able to do anything on mine until my father joins my brother in the afterlife."

"I'm not interested in building a bigger estate," Jack said.

"I'm not talking about the manor house. I mean the land. The tenants."

Jack frowned. "What's wrong with the tenants?"

Anthony smiled, but the expression didn't reach his eyes. "Their homes are falling apart; the money they earn from the estate isn't enough to support their families. And my good father refuses to put a penny into the cause. As your grandfather was my father's mentor, I can only assume your land is in a similar state of disrepair."

Jack shook his head. It was one more thing about his grandfather that disgusted him. Would the list never end? It seemed to grow exponentially every day. Perhaps, after the events over the next few weeks were concluded, he would take a trip back to the country estate and see about the tenants' condition. It was something productive on the horizon, and he felt his spirits lift ever so slightly.

He gave Anthony a half smile. "How much longer until you inherit, then?"

"Not much longer, according to my mother. My father grows crazier by the day—he shows all the symptoms of a disease my mother would rather not acknowledge. One he likely contracted from his many visits to town without her." Anthony paused, shaking his head. "Even if his body holds out, his mind is all but gone. I expect to hear from the family solicitor any day now."

"And if he is alive, but deemed unfit to carry out his duties as a peer, then you act in his place?"

Anthony nodded. "Much to my eternal regret. I was content to live the life of the younger son."

Jack nodded. "And I was content to live the life of the disinherited grandson."

"Why are you doing this, then?"

"For my mother and sister."

Anthony nodded. "Fair enough." He looked around the room for a moment. "Rousing card games usually pick up by evening."

Jack shook his head in bewilderment. "And in the meantime, this is the whole of it? They stand around talking about fashion with Mr. Brummell and make ridiculous bets in the book?"

Anthony Blake gave him a wide smile. "It's a gentleman's life, my friend. Who wouldn't want it?" He spread his arms out for emphasis.

"Ridiculous," Jack muttered.

"That it is. I have an appointment at Tattersall's to buy a horse. You're welcome to join me. Unless you'd rather compare notes with Beau."

Jack glanced again at Beau Brummell, who was showing his fans the finer details of his salmon colored waistcoat. "I do find it rather disturbing that he is the Prince Regent's bosom friend."

Anthony laughed and rose with a stretch. "If nothing else, England can rest assured that she will always be at the height of fashion. Which is a good sight better than being ruled by a mad king, wouldn't you agree?"

"Life is so much simpler at sea," Jack said as he stood and took another look around the room.

As they made their way to the door, Anthony stopped and pointed at a pedestal that held a large book. "Take a look," he said to Jack. "You'll find your own name in it."

Jack's brows pinched together as he examined the betting book; several of the entries were regarding him. How long he would remain at the earl's estate. How long until he returned to the sea and lost his inheritance. How much longer it would be until his life of leisure caused him to gain weight. And then how much weight he would gain.

As he turned to leave, he noticed several of the men in the group by the window watching him, likely hoping for a reaction of some sort. He cursed under his breath, knowing that Lady Ivy would have his head if he were to cause a scene out loud.

"Let's go buy a horse," he said to Anthony, and they left the building to its dandy inhabitants.

CHAPTER 14

Tea time can be a delightful occasion to renew acquaintances and form new ones. Care should be taken to insure the comfort of all of one's guests.

Mistress Manners' Tips for Every-day Etiquette

I vy was pressed for time, and her mother had suddenly become very interested in Ivy's life. It irked her to no end—especially given the fact that Ivy had tried to catch her attention for years—and to be inundated with questions when she was trying to leave the house and meet Jack at the maritime museum was most inopportune.

"I am helping Nana to ease the family's entrance into Society, Mama, and that is all." She tamped down an edge of extreme irritation that she knew was inappropriate to feel for one's mother. Ivy had hardened her heart against the woman; if Lady Imogene Carlisle didn't care to have a warm relationship with her daughter, so be it. Ivy found comfort in Nana, and it was enough.

Ivy took her pelisse from the butler with a smile of thanks and made her way to the front door.

"Ivy, I do think it unseemly for you to be spending so much time with the new earl, especially unchaperoned."

"We are never unchaperoned." Well, that might be stretching the truth a bit. But they weren't courting, for heaven's sake. She was his tutor. "And more often than not, Nana is with me." Hmm. That wasn't entirely true, either.

"I trust you understand, Ivy, the position you will put this family in if your behavior is anything but circumspect."

Ivy felt her nostrils flare and tried to tame her facial muscles into a mask of pleasantry. "Mama, you may trust me when I say that I am the last one you ever need worry over as it concerns good behavior. Caroline has made things difficult for all of us."

Imogene Carlisle flushed. "You needn't mention it, Ivy."

Of course. They never discussed Caroline because it was *unseemly*. Ivy's sister had always been self-absorbed, and Ivy had never enjoyed a warm relationship with her. Then Caroline's dalliance with a soldier had plunged the entire Carlisle family into a terrible state. And once, just once, she wanted her mother to show even the slightest bit of affection rather than censure. Ivy had received far more attention from her nannies than her mother. That wasn't unusual, she knew, but it had still stung.

"And you know I do not approve of so much time spent with your grandmother." Imogene's lips were pinched. She and the dowager countess, her mother-in-law, had never seen eye-to-eye. Ivy hated the tension that often accompanied Lady Olivia Carlisle's visits to her son and grandchildren. She found it far easier to leave the house to spend time with Nana.

"Nana is all things good and proper, Mama, and you needn't worry yourself on that count. Besides, I am a woman grown and am hardly going to be influenced at this point by someone else's negative behavior."

Imogene opened her mouth as though to rebut, but apparently thought better of it. "You will be home for dinner, then?"

Ivy nodded. "And if that changes, I will send word."

"Very well."

Ivy looked at Imogene for a moment longer before making her way outside. Ivy supposed her mother somehow equated affection with weakness. She was grateful beyond words for the close relationship she enjoyed with Nana. It was baffling, really, that her own father was nothing like his mother. In that regard, Ivy's parents were a perfect match. Stern, proper, stoic. And perhaps a little bland. Observing life through Jack's eyes had opened hers considerably. Small issues that had irritated her before had become significantly bothersome.

The ride to the maritime museum proved uneventful, and Ivy was glad to see Jack's tall frame near the entrance. My, but he was a handsome one. Once polished, he would make a young lady very happy by offering for her hand. Ivy felt a twinge of something near her heart but was unwilling to examine it further.

Jack surprised her when she met him at the entrance by taking her hand and bowing, placing a kiss upon her gloved knuckles. "My lady," he said with a ridiculous flourish.

"For heaven's sake," she said with a laugh, "we are not treading the boards! One might mistake you for a Shakespearean actor."

"Not at all." He offered his arm. "I merely seek to demonstrate the fruits of your labors."

She narrowed her eyes at him as they entered the building. "I do not trust you for a moment. I suspect you have an ulterior motive."

"On the contrary. Finally accepting my lot in life."

"Mmm-hmm."

They purchased tickets and began the stroll around the museum to different exhibits and artwork. They had gone along for some time in relative silence when Jack said, "Why, again, are you showing a sailor around the maritime museum?"

"I am thinking of ways to help you pass your time. A gentleman will often frequent museums, and this one seems particularly . . . manly."

"I do hate to disappoint, but I have lived most of my life at sea. Continual walks through this place will either bore me to tears or make me nostalgic to tears."

"Oh, dear." Ivy smiled. "It seems you are destined to cry either way. I find that most refreshing: a man who can show his true emotions without fear of appearing emasculated."

"If you find it refreshing, then I shall endeavor to weep each time we meet."

Ivy stopped their stroll and faced him, brows drawn. "Jack, truly, why the sudden change of heart?"

To his credit, he didn't try to pretend he didn't understand the question. "I've come to realize that the quicker I cooperate, the sooner I will see my mother and Sophia settled comfortably. I can then buy my own merchant vessel and return to the life I prefer."

Her heart skipped a beat, and she wasn't certain why. "But I thought we had agreed you need a bride and an heir," she said, looking up at his handsome face.

He shrugged. "I can still procure a bride and an heir. We are frequently in port—I will visit home when I can, and of course, my wife and child would be well provided for. It is one of the few good things about my suddenly deep pockets, I suppose."

Ivy chewed on her lip for a moment. "I don't imagine your bride will relish the thought of so much time apart from you."

"Lady Ivy," he said as he drew her hand through his arm and propelled her forward once again, "you have told me yourself that more marriages than not are lacking in any deep affection. I simply need someone who wants a title and money. The more I dwell upon the subject, the more I find that my plan would be a most suitable arrangement."

Ivy frowned.

"You can't think of any young women who are seeking marriage as a business transaction rather than a love match?" he pressed.

"You're a good man, Jack, with a good heart." Ivy tried to give voice to feelings that suddenly made no sense to her. It was true, she *had* told him that love matches were few and far between. So why, now, did the prospect of a loveless marriage based on nothing more than a few mutual goals seem so incredibly sad? "I suppose I had hoped for more for you."

He smiled at her in a manner that suggested brotherly affection, and it irritated her. "A very sweet sentiment, Lady Ivy, but highly unrealistic. I've accepted the fact that my parents' union was the exception, not the rule."

As they continued their walk through the museum, Ivy noted two things. The first was that he was incredibly knowledgeable on the subject of all things maritime, which she realized shouldn't have surprised her. The second was that she didn't care to ever visit it again. He was clearly in his element, and she found it utterly depressing that he should be kept from it. But the thought of him leaving London altogether, to return home only a couple of times per year for visits, depressed her further still. She would never see him at soirees, parties, balls, or other functions in which their circles ran.

But why that mattered, she couldn't imagine. He would belong to someone else.

They passed the better part of an hour, Jack defining and describing the items on display in such a way that Ivy found herself actually interested in what he said. When they left and stepped out again, she was surprised to hear Jack call out to someone on the street.

"Blake!"

Lord Anthony Blake paused and, with a smile, approached them.

"You know Lady Ivy Carlisle, I would imagine?" Jack said by way of introduction.

"I do indeed. My lady," Blake said with a short bow.

Ivy dropped into a curtsey with a smile. "I was not aware the two of you were acquainted." Lord Blake was quickly garnering himself a reputation as a bit of a wastrel, but she liked him. Heir to the Wilshire earldom, he was genuine and honest. And at a dinner a few months earlier, he had come to the defense of a frightened footman who had dropped a tray of food all over the ballroom floor. His compassion had impressed Ivy no end.

"I rescued him from White's," Blake said with a grin. "We purchased horses instead. He has told me you are showing him way of the elite. An admirable cause."

Jack snorted and Ivy laughed. "He is a very apt pupil." She glanced at Jack. "Before long, nobody will ever know he wasn't reared for the earldom from birth."

"Oh, dear lady, no. You will ruin him. You must turn him over to me."

At that, Ivy laughed harder. "My aim is to keep him respectable. You would be the one to ruin him, my lord."

"Psh," Blake said. "I would do nothing of the sort." He turned to Jack. "Check your stables, old man, and see if you need replacements. I'd be happy to join you at Tattersall's."

"I'll do that," Jack told him, and they bid their farewells. When they were out of earshot, Jack regarded her with brows raised. "You are friends, of a sort? That rather surprises me, my lady. Blake is a bit of a rascal."

"He is," she nodded and then smiled. "But he is a kind rascal. I like him."

"Perhaps you have your sights set on him, then?"

"Goodness, no." Ivy felt her face flush and hated it. "I am not entertaining any thoughts regarding any man at this time."

"Because your sister ruined the family reputation." His voice was flat.

"Yes, and we needn't discuss it further." Ivy heard her own mother's phrase even as she said it and winced slightly.

"It is ridiculous that you must pay for the sins of your sister."

Ivy agreed, but she kept it to herself. When she remained silent, he shrugged and took her umbrella, shielding her from the rain as they made their way out of the museum's shelter and toward the street.

Jack dropped Ivy by his mother's home after the visit to the museum. They had "womanly things" to discuss, she had said, and he didn't question it further. He figured he was much better off kept in the dark—it was a world entirely beyond his realm.

He decided to take Anthony Blake's advice and visit his stables. He knew next to nothing about horses, really, but he realized that if they were going to be a part of his life, perhaps he'd better learn. He had met the stable master briefly; Griffin was a hardened man who might have done well as a sailor, but there was something about his demeanor that Jack mistrusted. Perhaps Griffin was bitter about the old man's death, or maybe he felt Jack had no right to be the earl.

As he walked down the aisle in the stable, he began to wonder if perhaps he might need Blake's opinion after all. Everything seemed in tip-top condition, but what did he really know? As he neared the end of the row, Jack noted an older mare whose head drooped. He put his hand out to touch her nose, and the horse shied away with a start.

Talking to the animal as if trying to soothe a frightened child, he eventually gained enough of her trust to touch her gently without eliciting a startled reaction. He released her stall door and led her out into the aisle, noting several angry red marks about her flanks. His mind flashed to times aboard ship when discipline had been enforced—the appearance and demeanor of the horse mirrored that of sailors who had had the whip taken to them.

"What kind of trouble have you been in, little missy?" he murmured as he ran a gentle hand over the worst of the marks. She jerked away again at the touch, and he frowned.

"You there!"

Jack turned at the bark to see Griffin approaching him in angry strides. When the stable master recognized Jack, he slowed a bit but continued toward him.

"Didn't recognize yeh, m'lord," Griffin said. "Thought ye were a thief."

"If I were, Mr. Griffin, I would hardly choose this particular horse. Can you tell me how she came upon these wounds?"

Griffin's expression tightened. "She's stubborn, that one, and lucky I haven't sent her to the slaughterhouse."

"Might I assume she's also quite aged? Perhaps she would be better off at the country estate."

Griffin's eyes narrowed. "The old earl had no problem with the way I handled the stables."

Jack met the man's angry gaze and held it. "The old earl is dead now," he murmured, "and I do not much care about his preferences. I'll not have the animals abused."

Griffin flushed, the angry set of his jaw betraying his frustration. "Yer pardon, m'lord, but ye're a sailor. What do ye know of horses?"

"I know enough to insist that those I own not be beaten into submission. Training with fair methods is another matter altogether. Please send someone to fetch the veterinarian so that these wounds can be treated."

A muscle worked in Griffin's jaw, but he acquiesced with a quick bow. "M'lord," he said and left the stable in firm strides. Jack watched him leave, recognizing the sadistic vein he sometimes had seen aboard ship. There were those whose power over someone or something weaker manifested itself in very cruel forms.

Jack nudged the mare and returned her to her stall. Suspicious, he began examining each horse for signs of harsh treatment, and his anger grew. There were telltale marks on every animal, some bearing scars that had tried to heal but were visible upon closer inspection.

Jack summoned a stable boy and sent him with a message to Lord Anthony Blake. He wanted a second pair of eyes.

It wasn't the first thing Ivy would have listed on Things to Do with One's Afternoon, but she realized that tea with Clista Elliot was unavoidable for Sophia and Mary. It had to be done, and perhaps once would suffice.

Mary and Sophia had received the invitation from Clista the day before and had immediately contacted Ivy for her input. Ivy had spent the better part of that afternoon chatting with the two about what they might expect from Clista and how to best dodge any veiled barbs that might fly their way.

As they waited for the carriage to be brought around, Ivy considered the situation. Sophia had been a lady's maid in fine houses long enough to know how to sit, what to say, and how to eat and drink. Ivy wasn't worried about Sophia's abilities to dismiss Clista's nonsense. Mary also certainly possessed good manners, but Ivy became defensive in advance just thinking about the gentle woman getting her feelings hurt.

Ivy pasted a smile on her face as the carriage pulled up in front of Percival and Clista's home, and Sophia squeezed her mother's hand as the footman opened the carriage door and flipped down the steps. "We will stay only as long as we must," Sophia said. She had told Ivy that she wasn't certain she could hold her tongue if Mary were insulted outright.

Ivy took a deep breath as they entered the lavishly decorated town home, and upon entering the parlor was relieved beyond words to see

Nana already seated with a cup of tea in her hand. Ivy had mentioned the impending visit to Clista's the night before, and how Nana had secured an invitation without appearing gauche, Ivy would never know. Only she could have managed it. Ivy motioned for Mary to sit next to Nana, and Sophia took a seat on a settee next to Ivy.

There were five others in attendance in addition to Nana. Four of them Ivy knew from their association with her mother.

"I am surprised not to see the Misses Delaney and Lady Roose, Clista," one of the women said as the newcomers accepted cups of tea from the footman. "They never miss one of your teas."

Clista flushed slightly, her nostrils flaring just a bit before she smiled and offered a laugh. "They replied that they were unable to attend today," she said. "Life does get ever so busy as the Season progresses."

Mrs. Graston, seated to Ivy's immediate left, stirred her tea and nodded. Conversation picked up between two of the other guests, and Mrs. Graston leaned to Lady Hawthorne and murmured that Clista's invitations had been refused with more frequency after Percival had been disinherited in favor of the new earl.

A glance at Clista confirmed that she had also heard the comment, and Ivy's stomach clenched. How formidable an opponent would Clista be, Ivy wondered, if she were bitter enough?

Mrs. Graston turned her attention to Mary. "How are you settling in to your new accommodations, Mrs. Elliot?"

"Very well, thank you." Mary's voice was a bit thin. Ivy felt tension radiating off of Sophia in waves.

Nana smiled brightly at Mary and turned to Mrs. Graston. "Ladies, I would venture to guess that you are unaware we have an artist among us!"

Clista raised a brow. "Oh?"

Nana nodded and placed a hand on Mary's arm. "I have seen Mrs. Elliot's portfolio personally, and I must say I've not witnessed the likes of it in years. I have begged her shamelessly to allow me to host a showing for her, and she has finally consented. She is too modest, of course," Nana continued with a gentle laugh, "and paints for her own pleasure, but it is absolutely not to be missed, and I anticipate her first exhibition most anxiously."

There was an excited buzz then, and the women present turned to Mary with surprise and genuine interest. Ivy briefly closed her eyes and blessed the day Nana was born. Mary would be fine; she might even garner a reputation as a solitary, reserved artist. It would explain her shy nature and reluctance to be seen all over town as a woman recently stepped into a fortune.

Ivy felt Sophia relax next to her and glanced at her friend with a slight lift at the corner of her mouth.

"I do believe I love your grandmother," Sophia whispered as she lifted her teacup to her lips.

Conversation continued to swirl around the room and gradually turned to opinions on fine art and the artists who created it, but Ivy watched Clista discreetly and with a wary eye. Lady Hawthorne turned to Clista and asked after the welfare of Lady Finster, Clista's "bosom friend." Ivy heard Sophia clear her throat and recalled the humiliation Lady Finster had attempted to heap upon Sophia at the funeral.

Lovely, Ivy thought. She had quite forgotten that Clista Elliot and Lady Finster were so intimately connected. She would have to alert Nana to the situation and be certain they managed to keep a finger on any gossip that might spread before the Norringtons' ball, which was to occur in a few weeks' time. It was the perfect large social event of the Season for Sophia and Jack both to be officially seen, and if Ivy and Nana could manage to keep the bitter, sharp-tongued women in check they might just meet with success.

For the first time, Ivy wondered if it wouldn't be so much simpler to live a quiet life in the country tending sheep or milking cows. Animals tended to be easier to deal with than people.

CHAPTER 15

*To do something for another without expecting payment
in kind is the purest form of friendship.*

Mistress Manners' Tips for Every-day Etiquette

I vy scribbled the last of her notes for her next advice column and
checked her pocket watch, deciding the final draft would have to
wait. She and Sophia had an appointment downtown—Sophia had
a package to deliver to a friend and had asked Ivy to come along. As
she looked over her scribbles, she remembered the moment in Jack's
garden when he'd asked about the papers she carried around. It had
felt like a near miss that she had escaped without him discovering
she wrote incognito for a ladies' circular. Her anonymity was the one
thing that allowed her to continue writing the advice column. If her
identity were known, it would hardly be the thing for Society to realize she was engaged in an activity that *paid*.

She took a look around her bedroom—decorated in soft blues
and silvers—and reflected upon a lifetime of dreams to which the
walls had been witness. A perfect home, a perfect husband, perfect

children. She had envisioned such things as far back as she could remember, and Caroline's blunder had abruptly derailed all of it—or at the very least had postponed it. Ivy had also once been much more carefree with her joy, much less restrained in demeanor. When the family had come up against scorn and ridicule, she'd realized that all would be lost for her if she didn't rein her emotions firmly in.

And she was happy, for the most part, she told herself as she left her small writing desk and wandered to the four-poster bed. She wound her arm around one of the posts and turned her gaze to the window, which looked out over the picturesque square. So many dreams, hopes, plans—she had once been certain that everything she wished for would come to pass without question. And now she was the sister of a fallen woman, writing for pay, and training a toughened sailor in the ways of propriety. When had the world shifted so significantly? Was it inevitable? Was there anyone, really, whose dreams and goals actually came to fruition in the exact manner the dreamer had anticipated?

Shaking off her musings, she gathered a light shawl and her reticule and went downstairs to summon the carriage. Well-ordered, perfect on the surface; it was the way the Carlisle household had been managed since before Ivy had been born. But it was often cold. The bright spot, the warmth in her life, had always been Nana. Nana, who was anything but strictly conventional, who gently mocked Society behind its back and did as she pleased, but with style and class.

She exited the house and climbed into the carriage. It was rather unsettling to suddenly find herself dissatisfied with the life her mother had outlined for her. Thoughts of her future as she'd always envisioned it didn't feel as hopeful, somehow, and parts of her life that had become routine now seemed ridiculous and of little consequence.

She didn't *do* anything for anyone. She had tea and cakes, made calls, attended the theater, and anonymously gave advice to London's finest on how to behave properly. She thought of Jack muttering that there must be more to life, and for the first time in hers, she saw the truthfulness in the statement. Nobody had ever expressed such a sentiment to her, and now that it rattled around in her brain, she knew it would be impossible to shove it back into a corner.

Ivy was still deep in thought when the carriage pulled up in front of Mary and Sophia's home, and when Sophia climbed into the carriage, Ivy blinked and tried to bring her focus to the fore.

"My, but that seems some serious woolgathering," Sophia said as she settled in across from Ivy and the carriage began to move.

Ivy frowned and chewed on her lip. Her mother had often scolded her for gnawing on her lower lip, and she fought the impulse to immediately cease and desist.

"Are you ill?" Sophia tipped her head to the side and regarded Ivy.

Ivy smiled. "I am maudlin today, I suppose. Thinking of my future, wondering what it will hold. Wondering what I would like it to hold."

"A house with a wealthy husband, children, and a nanny—isn't that what we are supposed to strive for?" Sophia said, her smile softening the bite of her words.

"What did you hope for, before all of this?" Ivy asked her friend, motioning to the carriage with a sweep of her hand.

Sophia sighed and turned her gaze to the window. "I hoped to survive, to outlive my mother so that I would always be able to take care of her. A family of my own wasn't a dream I ever entertained. Mama gave her all for me, loved me, and worked so hard to provide for us that when she fell ill with consumption the first time, the effects weakened her physical state to the point that I don't believe she will ever be fully well."

"I never thought to say this, Sophia, but you are luckier than I."

Sophia turned to Ivy, one brow raised.

"You have a mother who loves you and expresses it. I had nannies who are long since gone and a mother who feels it a weakness to show affection."

Sophia watched Ivy with wise eyes, and Ivy wouldn't have been surprised to see that Sophia could read her mind. "What has happened, Ivy, with your Season? You ought to be making your own rounds right now, not helping misfits become Society darlings."

Ivy pursed her lips with a wince. She told Sophia of Caroline's indiscretions from beginning to end, leaving nothing out and feeling such a vast sense of relief at confiding in someone that it made her eyes sting with tears. "That I am not ruined entirely is a miracle in itself," she finished and dabbed at the corner of her eye. "And I find it vastly unfair, the more that time passes, that I am made to suffer for someone else's sins."

"Take comfort in the fact that your family is well enough established that you were able to weather the storm relatively unscathed," Sophia noted. She was astute and, of course, correct. Ivy felt foolish that her problems were of such little consequence compared to the trials Sophia and Mary had faced for years. And yet Sophia understood the depth of disgrace Caroline had wrought.

"And besides," Sophia added, "the *ton* is ridiculously shortsighted. You know full well that this Season's scandal is old news by the time the next one comes." Sophia paused for a moment. "Ivy, your defense of me at the graveside with Mrs. Finster—I am grateful beyond words. Nobody has ever done such a thing for me." Sophia flushed and looked away from Ivy. "Nobody aside from Mama and Jack has ever believed the best of me."

"Oh, Sophia," Ivy murmured. "Envy is a toxic thing. Most people would hardly believe that possessing beauty can be a heavy curse. Especially in a position of servitude to others who have fewer talents at their disposal. You carry yourself in such a way that your physical beauty is but icing on the cake. I am very glad that, for whatever reason, the old earl made things right."

Sophia shook her head with a rueful smile. "Poor Jack. This has battered his pride more than anything ever could have. But we have both agreed that we will do whatever is best for Mama. And I must selfishly admit, I've gained a perverse sense of satisfaction purchasing things for myself that the families for which I worked couldn't have afforded."

Ivy laughed and Sophia joined in. "I would say you've deserved every moment of that satisfaction," Ivy said. "It is long overdue."

Ivy told Sophia about her relationship with Nana as the carriage made its way across town and realized she'd never had a friend, a true friend, who listened and seemed to genuinely care. By the time the carriage came to a stop at the address Sophia had given the driver, Ivy felt significantly lighter in spirit.

"I have entirely monopolized all conversation," Ivy told Sophia as they stepped down from the carriage. "Tell me where we are and what we're going to do."

Sophia smiled. "We are here to deliver some clothes to a few friends of mine," she said as the footman retrieved a large portmanteau from the back of the carriage.

Ivy took in her surroundings, noting the close proximity to the docks and the suspicious glances she and Sophia received as people passed them on the street. Sophia indicated the rickety building before them. "This is where my mother and I used to live."

Ivy kept her mouth from dropping open, but only just. She had known that Sophia and Mary had lived in some degree of poverty, but the surroundings were horrific and her heart tripped as she thought of Mary Elliot, in her frail state, spending her days and nights in those rooms trying to keep her family alive doing piecework as a seamstress.

Sophia was watching Ivy carefully, likely judging her reaction. "Sophia," Ivy began, "I hardly know what to say. I am ashamed that this exists and I knew nothing of the particulars. I knew . . . but I didn't really, I suppose . . . know."

"What difference would it have made?" Sophia asked her.

"I don't know."

Sophia gave her a wry smile, absolving Ivy of guilt. "You can't singlehandedly save London."

Ivy's eyes clouded and stung, and not entirely from the soot and foul smell in the air. "It isn't right that I spend my time pursuing such mundane activities when this occurs under my very nose."

Sophia was quiet. She nodded once and then motioned with her head toward the front door. "I had hoped you might feel that way. I'm going to propose something to Jack, but I suspect it'll be an undertaking I can't handle entirely on my own."

"What is it you want to do?" Ivy asked as they drew closer to the building.

"I want to form a training school to equip women to go into service as housemaids, perhaps even ladies' maids. A home. But I would like to train women who have been forced into occupations rather . . . distasteful."

Ivy blinked, and she leaned a bit closer to Sophia. "You want to take prostitutes and transform them into housemaids?"

"Yes." Sophia didn't hesitate in her response. She said nothing further, didn't try to argue her case, and Ivy realized she didn't need to.

"I will help you any way I am able," Ivy said.

"It isn't a pretty sight," Sophia said, her brow raised, "and I imagine it will take some time before you are accustomed to interacting with people who have no concept of what your daily life is like."

Ivy stood a bit straighter. She was Olivia Knightley Carlisle's granddaughter. She could do anything. "I shall adjust," she told Sophia, who grinned widely at her. "Lead the way."

Ivy followed Sophia into the drafty and darkened interior of the decrepit building and climbed two flights of stairs before they finally came to a stop at one of four doors on the top level. Sophia knocked firmly, and they waited for what seemed an interminable amount of time before the door finally cracked open a sliver.

There was an audible gasp, and then the door was flung wide open. "Sophia!"

A woman who had likely seen fewer years than were manifested on her face clasped Sophia to her rail-thin frame and laughed. "An' look at you! All dolled up!"

"Gilly, this is my friend Lady Ivy Carlisle, and we are bringing you and the others some clothing."

Gilly looked at Ivy with wariness, and Ivy offered a smile, hoping to put the woman at ease—or at least to stem some of the mistrust.

Gilly fidgeted a bit and said to Sophia, "I haven't prepared anything for tea." Sophia waved a hand at her. "And the others are out . . ."

"We don't expect tea, silly. But do take these." Sophia handed

Gilly the portmanteau and smiled. "There are enough gowns in here for the four of you, and they are practical but certainly well enough made that they'll last for some time."

"I don't like charity," Gilly said, taking the portmanteau with a longing in her face that was at odds with her statement.

"It isn't charity," Sophia said. "It's payment for the kindness you've always shown to me and Mama." Sophia cleared her throat and shook her head slightly. "At any rate, Gilly, I will return again soon, and in the meantime, be safe. Tell the others hello from me and from Mama."

Gilly stood uncertainly in the doorway and Ivy glanced at Sophia, who seemed equally confused. Her worlds had collided, and Ivy wondered if Sophia was at a loss as to which identity belonged to her.

Gilly looked at Ivy, who extended her hand to the woman. "It was a pleasure to meet you, Gilly," Ivy told her and shook her hand slightly when Gilly seemed disinclined to do anything with it.

"And you," Gilly said.

"I included some bread and cheese in the bag as well," Sophia told Gilly. "Also a card with my new address. Please send word if you need anything."

Gilly's eyes filmed over and she nodded. "Thank you," she said and pulled Sophia forward in another embrace before backing into the apartment and closing the door. Sophia stared at the closed door for a moment, then turned her attention to one farther down the hall. She pointed to it and murmured, "That is where Mama and I lived."

Ivy couldn't imagine how frail, little Mary had survived as long as she had. She didn't say as much to Sophia, but she wondered if Mary's love for her child had propelled her forward each day.

"Do you want to look at it?" Ivy asked Sophia.

"No. I've seen it enough."

Ivy followed Sophia's lead, and they stood in the hallway for a few more moments before finally making their way down the stairs and back outside.

CHAPTER 16

The call to do something greater than oneself
should be heeded without delay.
Mistress Manners' Tips for Every-day Etiquette

Jack sat back in the lavish leather chair that graced the earl's library—*his* library—and stared at Clarence Fuddleston for a long
moment before trusting himself to speak. "Are you telling me that
money has been disappearing from my grandfather's coffers for two
years? How was this never noticed?"

Fuddleston shook his head and removed his spectacles, polishing
them with a handkerchief before perching them back on his nose.
"Blackington handled the books for your grandfather's estate for fifty
years before he died two years ago. Stallings has maintained them
since, and, after this discovery, I believe we should review everything
with a fine-tooth comb. Had you not asked me about recent horse
purchases, we might never have known."

"Am I to assume, then, that the stable master and the accountant have been working together to rob the estate?" Jack envisioned tying both men to the mast and extracting his pound of flesh with a whip.

Fuddleston met Jack's gaze with frank regard, his eyes blinking owlishly from behind his round spectacles. "It would appear so, my lord. I'm afraid your grandfather never asked me to look into the finances— and I'll admit, I never thought there would be cause to do so."

Jack had spent the bulk of his adult life in close association with other men and had developed a keen ability to read their intentions. He studied the little man quietly for a moment, noting that Fuddleston did not fidget under his scrutiny. "I should like you to assume the position, Fuddleston, if you've an interest in it."

Fuddleston blinked. "The position, sir?"

"Of stable master."

Fuddleston's mouth hung slack, and Jack found he couldn't maintain a stern expression. He smiled. "I jest, good man. I extend the position of accountant, solicitor, and my personal man of affairs. I need someone I can trust, as I am swimming about in a sea of confusion most of my time here in London."

Fuddleston closed his mouth, brows raised high. After a moment or two of silence, he nodded once, definitively. "I accept, my lord. Most gratefully."

"You will take a day or so to alert your other clients, I would assume? I'll pay you handsomely to work exclusively for this estate. Provided there's any money left after those scurvy rats leave."

Fuddleston's lips twitched. "As far as I can discern, the missing amounts are minimal."

"But then, I suppose it is the principal of the thing, is it not?"

"Most definitely, my lord. Their actions are reprehensible." Jack's new accountant nodded and lifted his chin a notch. Of one thing

Jack was certain: Clarence Fuddleston might be an odd duck, but he would be a man of integrity to the day he died.

After excusing himself, Jack made his way through the town house and out to the mews with a mind bent on murder. By the time he found the object of his quest, he was near to boiling over. The stable master watched him approach with something resembling a sneer, which he smoothed over with what seemed considerable effort.

"Griffin," Jack said, his voice deadly calm, "you're fired." If he hadn't been so angry, he might have found humor in the man's stunned expression.

Griffin opened his mouth and closed it a few times before finally sputtering, "I know the stable, m'lord, and it'd be a mistake ye're makin' to let me go."

Jack studied the man for a long moment, long enough that Griffin finally shifted under his scrutiny. "I have proof positive, Mr. Griffin, that you have been stealing from this estate. Given that, coupled with the fact that you abuse the horses, I see absolutely no reason not to dismiss you. You're fortunate I'm not having you thrown into prison, which I'm still of a mind to do if you don't vacate immediately and never return."

Griffin's nostrils flared, although his expression had paled considerably. "Ye don't belong here," he finally exploded. "Ye're the laughingstock of the whole town."

"And you would know this because you move in such illustrious circles, I presume." Jack drew upon the few memories he had of his father and tried to channel his stature and confidence. It helped alleviate some of the insecurity he felt at Griffin's insult. It didn't help matters much that Griffin probably *had* heard such things—gossip amongst servants always flowed in a steady stream. Even Jack knew that much.

Griffin glared at Jack before turning and making his way to the back room. Jack watched as the door slammed shut and wondered if the man would be foolish enough to cause problems. A sound just behind him interrupted his musings, and he turned to see Pug standing there, his features tense.

"Is it true, then?" Pug asked. "Griffin is leaving?"

Jack frowned and turned his full attention to the boy. "He is," Jack told him. "What of it, Pug?"

Pug shrugged, and Jack recognized the attempt to feign nonchalance. "No reason."

"Has there been a problem?" Jack asked.

"No." Pug looked at a spot just beyond Jack's shoulder and shrugged again. His refusal to meet Jack's eyes had always been a telling response.

Jack inched closer and placed a hand on Pug's shoulder, determined to hide his rising anxiety from the boy. "What has he done to you?"

Pug shook his head. "Nothin'. Just smacked me around some."

Jack's anger surged and he tamped it back down. "Are you certain that was all?" Jack had made a point of drilling into his sailors the fact that Pug was not to be molested in any way. Young, defenseless boys were often a target of the depraved. That the boy might have to fear the same thing in his new life did not sit well with Jack.

Pug nodded and finally looked up at Jack. "Truly. That's all."

Jack squeezed the boy's shoulder a bit. "He's leaving, at any rate. And you'll tell me if you encounter issues with anyone else." He smiled, trying to lighten the mood. "Nobody is allowed to 'smack you around' but me. Is that understood?"

Pug grinned and ducked his head. "Yes, sir."

Jack heard the back door open again and turned as Griffin stormed his way out of the stables, casting a dark glance at both Jack and Pug as he left. Pug inched closer and Jack put an arm about his shoulders.

"That's the last of him." Jack gave the boy one final pat. "You go on into the house and eat your lunch. Then I'll be needing you to straighten my cravats, or do whatever it is that valets do."

Pug grinned again and saluted before running off. Jack watched the empty space for a moment before drawing his brows together in thought. He couldn't very well be with the boy every minute of the day, but he didn't like the fact that Pug had experienced trouble and Jack had been none the wiser. Pug wasn't a sheltered lad—he'd spent a good portion of his young life aboard ship with some of the roughest men life had to offer. For him to have been afraid of Griffin spoke volumes.

Jack made his way back to the office to draft an official letter of dismissal for the accountant and decided that after firing his second employee of the day, he would stop by Anthony Blake's residence to see if his new friend could recommend a good stable master.

Ivy sat with her parents in the family dining room and spooned some fruit into her mouth, chewing carefully and trying to act as though they weren't staring at her.

"You want to fund a *what?*" her mother said, quiet.

Ivy fought a wince; when her mother was displeased, she was quiet.

"A reformation home for wayward girls," Ivy said, her tone light. "A training program for housemaids."

Ivy's father regarded her with brows raised but remained silent.

"Ivy, that is quite possibly the most ridiculous bit of nonsense you've concocted to date," her mother said, turning her attention to her food.

Ivy felt her face heat. "It is a most worthy cause."

"And you would then peddle these girls out to our friends? Suppose one of them robs the house or assaults a family member?"

Ivy couldn't imagine for the life of her why a young girl seeking employment as a housemaid would assault a family member, but she bit back a retort. It wouldn't do to be sassy with her mother. For one, it was improper. For two, Mama had a way of making things difficult.

"With training, such things should not occur," Ivy said. "It is an excellent solution to one of London's most plaguing problems."

"And it is not for us to dirty our hands with," her mother said. "We will not throw money at a scandalous project doomed to fail."

Ivy took a breath and briefly closed her eyes. "I do not believe it is doomed to failure. And your friends would be most impressed at your charity."

"We will speak no more of it."

And with that, the subject was closed.

Ivy finished the rest of the meal in silence, her frustration reaching new heights with each tick of the large clock in the hallway. Her eyes burned with tears she knew she could not allow escape, and she kept them open wide as she stared at her plate, willing the moisture to recede. Against her will, one tear escaped and trailed down her cheek, and she fought back a sniffle. It had always been her curse; Ivy's emotional outlet was tears—tears of anger, joy, sadness—and that was extremely inconvenient when living with a woman who preferred to show no emotion at all.

"Pull yourself together, Ivy," her mother said as she signaled for the footman to clear her dishes. "Frankly, I'm surprised at you. I cannot imagine what has gotten into your head—you know very well that what you do now will affect the success of your Season. You do not have the luxury of playing do-gooder to a band of unfortunates."

"Caroline made certain of that, didn't she?" Ivy said and very nearly clapped her hand over her mouth.

Her mother's lips tightened, and Ivy's father sat, as always, silent. "We will *not* speak of it," her mother said in icy tones that brooked no argument.

"I should like to be excused," Ivy murmured, not meeting her mother's eyes for fear that her own would give away her anger.

Her father nodded his assent, and Ivy left the dining room. She dashed upstairs to her bedroom, grabbed her writing portfolio and reticule, and hurried back down the stairs to the front door, where she gave instructions for a carriage to be brought around. After telling the driver to take her to her grandmother's house, she sat back into the carriage and allowed her tears free reign, hoping she would be able to disguise all evidence of them by the time she reached Nana's.

It was not to be. Although she did a fair job of mopping her face up with a lacy handkerchief, the moment she saw her grandmother in the sitting room, she dissolved into tears all over again. It took several fits and starts, but she eventually poured her heart out onto her grandmother's shoulder as the older woman held her close and patted her back.

"I'm tired of paying for Caroline's mistakes," she cried. "And we don't even know where she is! My parents do not care one whit for her welfare, and I just realized today, we have no earthly idea where she is. Our own flesh and blood!"

"Caroline is well enough," Nana said, and Ivy lifted her head to look at her.

"Do you know for certain?"

"Of course. I know exactly where she is. Did you think I would leave her to the wolves? I daresay it might be just a matter of time before the ne'er-do-well abandons her, but she is physically safe, at least."

Ivy's tears flowed again. "You see? You've taken the time to see that she's well. My own parents could not care less about her. And she may well end up like Gilly and the others—they need help immediately, and my parents refuse to offer it!"

"Gilly?" Olivia's brows drew together.

Ivy told her about the visit she'd made with Sophia and of Sophia's intentions to create a training school and home for young women who had fallen upon hard times. "And my mother refuses to lend a shilling to the cause," she finished and pounded a fist against her thigh. "She is more concerned with keeping up appearances than with doing good for those who are forced to do unspeakable things just to eat!"

Nana cupped the side of Ivy's face with her hand and smiled. "And there is my Ivy," she said and rubbed her thumb along Ivy's cheek. "The spirited little one I used to know."

"Does me absolutely no good," Ivy grumbled and wiped again at her eyes.

Nana produced a handkerchief, and Ivy attempted to dry her

tears for the second time. "Oh, I wouldn't say that," Nana said with a chuckle. "A determined force can change the world."

"If the force's mother approves." Ivy rolled her eyes, feeling very much like a pouty child.

Nana sobered and held Ivy's face in her hands. "I will help fund the project."

"Really?" Drat, the tears reappeared with a vengeance.

"Truly." Nana nodded and gave Ivy a gentle smile.

"I don't know that we will need it," Ivy admitted, "as Sophia will propose it to Jack, and I daresay he has enough capital for a hundred such endeavors, but I should very much like to be a part of it. I want to do something . . . amazing. To make a difference. Not just handing out advice on proper behavior."

Nana clasped Ivy's hands in her own and gave them a squeeze. "Nothing you have done to date has been a waste," she said. "The skills you possess will be more useful now than ever. If we want these young women to succeed, they will need to learn everything you have to teach them."

Ivy nodded and tried to stop sniffling. It was most unbecoming. "I do believe I am gaining more from this experience with the Elliots than they are."

Nana kissed Ivy's cheek and gave her hands a final squeeze before standing. "I daresay it is entirely mutual." Something in the woman's eyes gave Ivy pause.

"You are plotting something nefarious, Nana."

"I would never. Come, now, and let us pay a visit to Mary Elliot. I must speak with her regarding an art showing."

"You have that look about you," Ivy said as she stood and smoothed her dress. Wiping her eyes a final time with the handkerchief, she glanced at her grandmother, who was the very picture of innocence.

"I've no idea what you mean."

"It is the same look you wore for a week before you tricked me into writing a column for pay."

"And that has been very good for you," Nana said with a wink. "I don't regret it for a moment."

CHAPTER 17

If a friend should fall ill, sometimes the best
course of action is to simply offer support.
Mistress Manners' Tips for Every-day Etiquette

A week had passed since Jack had relieved Griffin, the stable master, and Stallings, the accountant, of their duties, and life seemed to be running relatively smoothly. Pug and Millie, the irreverent maid, formed an odd friendship, and Jack was glad for it. The girl had taken on an elder-sister role with the boy, and although he pretended irritation, Pug lit up when he saw her. Jack had arranged for a tutor to work with the boy four days a week. Pug was less than thrilled with the new routine, but he laughed when Jack threatened to throw him overboard if he try to skip his lessons.

As for Jack's part, he was a bit more at ease with the nearly constant presence of Clarence Fuddleston, who was, oddly enough, a calming influence on his nerves. Just when he thought he might have a decent handle on the ridiculous earl business, something would inevitably surface to throw him again into the dark. One thing was becoming clear—if an earl wanted to take a hand in day-to-day matters rather than merely turn things over to the solicitor or accountant, there was certainly enough to keep him busy.

When Jack and Fuddleston had reviewed the books, they had uncovered enough discrepancies to necessitate Stalling's arrest; the bulk of the stolen funds were nonrecoverable, but thankfully he had been altering the ledgers in small enough amounts that the estate was not bankrupt. Far from it, in fact. Jack had been forced, more than once, to consciously close his dropped-open mouth as he reviewed his assets with Fuddleston, who handled the whole of it without batting an eye. Of course the little man would be used to staring at such huge amounts; he had worked for the upper classes his entire adult life. Jack had the satisfaction, only once, of catching Clarence off guard—when he proposed a salary that was clearly above and beyond anything the man was expecting.

Reflecting on the rapid changes his life had taken, Jack relaxed one evening in the dressing room that adjoined his bedroom and propped his feet on a footstool next to the fireplace. It was warm and comfortable; he had just finished a good meal after spending the day on the back of a horse, which would most certainly have him sore by morning. He had ridden a few times in his life, enough to have a rudimentary feel for it, but the lessons Lady Ivy was insisting upon were more grueling than he would ever have anticipated. She maintained that when hunting season rolled around and he was at the country estate with his family, it would be quite the thing to invite at least a dozen of their closest friends—of which they currently had none, he had pointed out—to spend a fortnight enjoying games, food, and the traditional fox hunt. He would be ill equipped as the lord of the manor if he could not ride well, and how would his mother and Sophia fare in Society if he so clearly lacked the necessary social graces?

Jack closed his eyes, a half-drunk glass of port in his hand, and reflected on Lady Ivy's activities of the past week. She had been a flurry of energy, inviting Mary and Sophia to his home so that they might all review peerage, which had bored Jack nearly to tears. She had invited them daily to tea and had accepted their invitations on Jack's behalf to join them for tea at their house. She instructed him continually on his table manners, watching him like a hawk so that he was very nearly ready to stop eating in her presence altogether, but he felt absurdly pleased when he did something that met her satisfaction and she gave a slight nod of approval.

She had an intensity of late that he sensed stemmed from her burgeoning project with Sophia as they developed plans for their boarding school for young women who needed a boost. When Sophia had first approached him with the idea, he had not been at all surprised that his sister would want to pursue such an endeavor. When she had told him that Lady Ivy was to be her partner, however, he had been stunned. The more he observed her, though, the more he realized she was certainly equal to the task. If he weren't careful, he might start to admire Lady Ivy much more than was wise.

He winced a bit as a twinge of pain caught him across the midsection, and he wondered when his pleasantly sleepy state had given way to a slight sense of nausea. With a frown, he opened his eyes and sat up straight in his chair, bending slightly as another spasm of pain shot through his stomach.

Hastily setting his drink on the side table at his elbow, he stood and paced for a moment, removing the cravat from where it hung loosely about his neck and eventually shedding his shirt altogether. It was warm in the room, too warm, and it wasn't long before he lunged for the washbasin on his dressing table and lost his dinner completely.

Something wasn't right. He'd had food poisoning before, and raging illnesses with fevers that had left him bedridden on the stormy seas for days. His current state was different, and he made his way back to the side table where he'd set his glass of port. Barely keeping his grip on it when another shooting pain had him nearly bent in half, he noted through squinted eyes the presence of a fine film that had settled along the bottom—granules of some sort that clung to the side of the glass when he tipped it slightly.

"Pug!" he called out and was relieved when the boy quickly made an appearance from the adjoining valet's room.

"Sir?" Pug's eyes widened as he crossed the room and made his way to Jack's side.

"Have Mrs. Harster send for the doctor," he managed and wondered if he was going to lose whatever might still be left of his dinner all over Pug's shoes.

Pug ran for the door, but at Jack's yell, he halted at the door frame. "Sir?"

"Get Lady Ivy."

By the time Ivy arrived at the earl's town house, she was tied in knots wondering what she might find. She had left Jack to return to her home only two hours before; Pug's cryptic message that the earl had fallen ill and needed her right away had her baffled.

She arrived at Jack's home to find Mrs. Harster wringing her hands and Watkins looking rather pale. "What has happened?" she asked as she doffed her pelisse and handed it, along with her bonnet and gloves, to Watkins.

"I do not understand it," the woman said. "He was fine at dinner, you saw him, my lady . . ."

Ivy nodded. "Where is he? Have you sent for the doctor?" She moved toward the staircase and began climbing when Mrs. Harster nodded and gestured to the second floor.

"Dr. Featherstone should be here in a few minutes. He doesn't live far away," Mrs. Harster said, and Ivy wondered if the woman were going to dissolve into tears.

How bad could it be, really? Ivy climbed the stairs quickly and hurried down the hallway to the earl's suite. The door to his dressing room was ajar, and she spotted Pug standing near the hearth, his eyes wide and face pale.

"Lady Ivy!" he said, rushing to her side. "He's awful sick."

Ivy put a hand on Pug's shoulder, which was very nearly the same height as her own. "We will find the cause, Pug. Never fear." She paused for a moment, wondering what course of action to take. She had certainly never entered a man's bedchamber before, and to do so when he was ill was a concept utterly foreign.

She thought of what Nana would do in such circumstances, and she remembered her grandmother sitting by the old earl's side as he *died*, for heaven's sake. Squaring her shoulders, she walked across the dressing room and peeked inside the bedroom. The sight of the big man doubled over on the floor at the side of his bed was jarring, and she rushed to him.

"Jack," she murmured and placed a hand on his back.

Sweat dripped from his brow, and he clenched his fists at his stomach. Without looking at her, he ground out, "You shouldn't be in here."

"You sent for me," she said and rubbed her hand between his shoulder blades.

He nodded. "If something happens to me, I need you to care for my family. Percival will inherit and he . . ."

Ivy shook her head. "Do not even speak of it, Jack. The doctor is coming and you will be well straight away."

Jack glanced at her as a spasm of pain crossed his features. "Someone has poisoned me, Ivy. I saw it in the glass of port. Retrieve it before someone clears it out of the dressing room."

Ivy's heart tripped as she stared for a moment at Jack, her eyes widening as comprehension dawned. "Oh, mercy," she whispered.

"Go." He motioned with his head to the doorway and Ivy shot to her feet, rushing into the other room and looking frantically until she saw the half-drained glass of port on the side table. With trembling fingers, she picked it up and carried it back into Jack's bedroom, setting it carefully on the bedside table behind him.

Dropping down next to him again, she wrapped her hands around his arm. "Let's get you up into bed," she said. "The doctor will be able to help you soon." Biting her lip, she shifted and slid her arm under his, lifting against his weight and realizing there was no possibility of hefting him into the bed without his assistance.

"Jack," Ivy grunted as he shifted his weight and she strained for all she was worth, "did you, by chance, rid yourself of the contents of your stomach?"

He glanced at her then, and she caught a tiny glimpse of his subtle mockery to which she had become so accustomed. "You mean, did I throw up all over the dressing room?"

"For heaven's sake," she muttered as he lifted one leg up onto the high mattress with a grunt. "Why must it be 'all over the dressing room'? I certainly do not care one whit where you did it."

"Yes," he groaned as she gave him a shove and lifted his boot onto the bed, registering the fact that his leg probably weighed more than she did. "I did rid myself of the contents of my stomach, and hopefully most of the poison."

"Who served you the drink?" Ivy asked, her mind spinning as she looked at the glass sitting so innocently on the bedside table.

He shrugged and lay down on his side, facing her and pulling his knees up as he hugged his midsection. "One of the maids, I suppose. I told Mrs. Harster I would take my port up here, and I was in the dressing room when it was delivered."

Ivy frowned and placed her hands on her hips, thinking. "I cannot imagine who in the household would benefit from your . . ." she glanced at Jack, not wanting to finish her thought.

"Percival benefits. He must have paid someone," Jack said, his eyes closed.

Ivy looked at the door, feeling helpless. She needed Nana. "Where is that doctor?" she fretted, knitting her brows together.

"Don't let him bleed me," Jack groaned.

"Pardon me?" Ivy looked at him in alarm.

"Do not let him anywhere near me if he has leeches."

Ivy felt her own stomach twist. Perhaps she would lose the contents of her stomach along with the earl. Feeling slightly dizzy, she leaned her hip against the bed and stared down at the big sailor who lay like a child in the bed.

"Shall I send for your mother and Sophia?" she asked him quietly.

"No." The response was quick and definitive. "I'll not have them see me like this."

Ivy narrowed her eyes slightly, not certain if she should be flattered or offended that he didn't care if she saw him in that state.

"Jack," she finally said, moving closer to him, "I am so far out of my element. I don't know what to do for you."

He grabbed one of her hands in response and gripped it firmly, saying nothing. And with that, she waited by his side for several more long minutes until the doctor finally entered the room, followed by a flustered Mrs. Harster.

CHAPTER 18

To discover the goodness done by a friend
for others is a treasure to be cherished.

Mistress Manners' Tips for Every-day Etiquette

Ivy went downstairs to the parlor after the doctor proclaimed Jack ill but not in imminent danger of death. It was fortunate he *had* thrown up before the poison had worked its way into his system completely. He would be weak for a few days, but he would recover. The doctor examined the glass of port, touching the tip of his finger to the residue in the glass and tasting it, and suggested it was likely strychnine.

The hour was long past midnight, and yet the shadowy corners and spaces below stairs echoed with occasional whispers. A good portion of the household knew what had happened, of course, and Ivy had no doubt that the rest of London would by noon as well.

Mrs. Harster was a nervous wreck, her face pale and her fingers tied in knots. "I can't imagine who'd a done such a thing, my lady," the woman said, her voice shaking. "The earl'll turn us all out by this time tomorrow, fer sure."

"Nonsense." Ivy felt the fatigue settle in behind her eyes now that the worst of the emergency had passed. "I am certain we will get to the bottom of the matter. We'll find the one responsible and that will be that."

The older woman's eyes widened. "Who would do this?"

Ivy regarded her for a moment, wondering at the best course of action. A name flashed into her mind, and she seized on it. "Perhaps Lord Anthony Blake can be of some help to us," she suggested. "He is one of his Lordship's closer acquaintances. We will discuss it tomorrow. I shall want to speak with all the servants then."

Mrs. Harster's face whitened even more dramatically, and she put a hand to her heart. She nodded and backed out of the room.

Ivy sat pensively near the cold fire at the hearth. A few things were becoming clear to her, not the least of which was the fact that Jack needed to immediately reassign his heir. It wouldn't surprise Ivy in the least to find Percival and Clista behind the poisoning stunt, and if they were out of the line of inheritance entirely, it might remove the temptation to kill the current earl. People would talk, of course, and it might be considered mildly scandalous, but the thought of Percival having any sort of control over Mary and Sophia if Jack were dead was alarming.

She laughed aloud at the thought of Jack assigning Pug as his heir, but sobered when she considered how quickly the boy would be dispatched if such were the case. No, the heir would need to be someone robust and with a certain amount of political and social clout. She would speak with Jack in a few hours, after he had had some rest.

Deciding to check on Jack, she climbed the stairs to the second floor, deep in thought. The doctor entered the dressing room from Jack's bedroom just as Ivy entered from the hallway. The little man's bald pate shone in the lamplight, and he wiped at his forehead with a handkerchief.

"How is the earl, then?" Ivy asked him as he pocketed the fabric and snapped the buckle on his medical bag.

"He is resting," the doctor told her. "I did not administer laudanum, as it might interact with any lingering poison still in his system, so his sleep may be fitful. It's unfortunate but necessary."

Ivy eyed the medical bag with a raised brow.

"Is there a problem, my lady?"

"Did you . . . that is . . . do you carry leeches with you, doctor?" She felt nearly faint merely asking the question.

He drew his brows together behind his spectacles and shook his head as he made his way toward the door. "As it happens, I do not have a fresh batch at my home. A pity—it would have undoubtedly drawn the poison out more quickly. As it is now, he will have to sweat it out."

Ivy felt a sense of relief at his statement and nodded, trying to maintain what she hoped was a regretful expression. "Thank you, then," she said as he left the room.

Uncertain, she looked for a moment at the bedroom door, which stood slightly ajar. There was a soft glow coming from within, and she crept to the doorway, peeking inside at the bed.

"Pug?" Jack's voice was thready, and it alarmed her.

"No, it's Ivy." She moved tentatively into the room and approached the bed. The doctor had apparently helped Jack into a nightshirt and settled him under the covers. He was sweating profusely, and Ivy frowned, remembering the doctor's words. His body was expelling the poison, which was what it needed to do. As she observed him, however, she couldn't help but draw back the heavy coverlet. She shifted the thin sheet about his shoulders, and he sighed softly.

"That is much better." He cracked his eyes open. "I am so thirsty."

Ivy found a fresh pitcher of water on the washstand and poured him a glass. Holding it to him, she moved closer when she realized he didn't have the strength to grasp it himself. He raised himself up enough to take a sip as she positioned the glass at his lips, then lowered his head to the pillow.

"I thought perhaps I might contact Lord Anthony Blake," Ivy told him softly. "We will discover who has done this to you."

"You will care for my mother and Sophia?" he murmured.

"Of course. They will be fine. And when you are well, we will discuss . . . things."

"What sort of things?" He cracked open his eyes again and winced at the light. Ivy reached over to the bedside lamp and turned the flame down until it was barely glowing.

"Business matters," she said.

"Ivy, I am . . . I cannot defend myself tonight. Send Pug in here, will you?"

Her heart melted a bit at the thought of the big sailor defended by a wiry twelve-year-old boy. "Certainly I will. Is there anyone else you trust to be with you, perhaps someone a bit . . . bigger?"

"Pug is fierce enough when provoked," Jack said. "But I suppose Fuddleston would be my second choice."

Ivy raised her brows sky-high and choked back a laugh. Fuddleston? The man was scarcely larger than Pug and likely much less fierce. She drew in a breath to compose herself and let it back out again. "Of course. I shall summon Pug and Fuddleston."

"Fuddleston is here in the house . . ." he said, his words fading.

"I'm sorry?"

"I gave him a room. He was boarding with another man who . . . bathe . . ."

"What? Who bathed?" Ivy leaned closer to hear him.

"Didn't like to bathe. Made Fuddleston nauseous."

Ivy looked at the lamp for a moment, wondering if Jack were delirious. "You gave your solicitor a room in your house because he boarded with a man who didn't bathe and made him nauseous?"

" . . . tired, Lady Ivy, and feeling the urge . . . be sick again."

"How on earth has he slept through the ruckus?" Ivy wondered aloud.

" . . . sound sleeper . . . bang on the door to rouse him."

Stunned, Ivy slowly turned from the bed and made her way out of the room. What sort of man found comfort in protection from a cabin boy and sought to ease his solicitor's discomfort by giving him accommodations in his own home? She crossed the dressing room to the other side, where she knew Pug occupied the valet's smaller quarters. The sort of man, she answered her own question, who was not raised in privilege and judged all of humanity equally. Knocking on the door, she waited until she heard a rustle on the other side and Pug cracked it open.

"My lady?" he murmured, rubbing his eyes.

"Your master needs the comfort of your protection tonight, Pug. Gather a few blankets to make a pallet on the floor by his bedside."

The boy stood up straighter. "He asked for me?"

She nodded. "He trusts you."

In a matter of moments, Pug had gathered blankets and made his way across the dressing room to Jack's bedroom. When Ivy sleepily exited into the hallway, she heard the snap of blankets as Pug made his bed. Deciding she would feel no stranger about the evening as a whole than if she awoke one morning in the wilds of Africa, she descended the stairs to look for Mrs. Harster, who could then send a servant to awaken Mr. Fuddleston. The rattled housekeeper managed to mask her surprise when Ivy told her the solicitor was to sleep on the sofa in the earl's dressing room—or perhaps she had no surprise left to feel in the wee hours of a very odd night.

By the time Ivy's carriage pulled up in front of her family home, she had decided she would sleep as late into the morning as she could manage and cancel the earl's scheduled lessons on Advanced Breakfast Etiquette.

Chapter 19

If an action is perceived as an offense, the best response is to act as though nothing untoward has occurred.

Mistress Manners' Tips for Every-day Etiquette

Jack stood in the doorway of his home's music room and glared at Ivy. She had allowed him four full days in his sickbed before demanding he resume his lessons in Upper-Crust Stupidity. "I do not need to dance," he barked and cast a warning glance at Pug, who snorted behind his sleeve and coughed to cover it.

Ivy turned away from the window that overlooked the back gardens. "Your mother and Sophia are on their way," Ivy told him with a smile, "and they were ever so glad to hear you're well enough to resume your studies. We are borrowing Pug and Mr. Fuddleston, who has assured me he will arrive as soon as he finishes this morning's correspondence."

"I am not feeling well enough for such rigorous activity," Jack said, although it was stretching the truth. He didn't feel just the thing yet, but truthfully he could have been up and about the day before.

"It will not be rigorous." Ivy approached him with that expression she often wore—the one she used to argue with him and more often than not emerge victorious. She laid a hand on his arm as he shot her a look through half-lidded eyes.

"It will be more rigorous than my current state will support."

"I have it on good authority that you took a lengthy stroll last night." She looked up at him with an innocent blink. Her eyes were a distinct shade of green today, and he realized the color varied in intensity depending on what she wore. He wondered why he'd never noticed it before. Her hair, the color of dark honey, was curled to perfection as always, and he imagined it would feel soft between his fingers.

Shaking his head, he scowled a bit. He figured the poison must have addled his brain. When he'd decided to enjoy the time spent in the company of the pretty young woman, he hadn't thought to become genuinely enamored of her.

Ivy waved a hand in playful dismissal and cast a grin at him as she turned and made her way toward the center of the room, where she beckoned to Pug. "You must learn the fundamentals," she said to Jack as Pug joined her warily. "You'll soon be courting London's finest, and you'll not want to make a fool of yourself."

"I'll not be courting London's finest," he muttered. "This is an utter waste of time, and Fuddleston and I have a mountain of work today."

"Your Lordship," she said as she curtseyed deeply and motioned for Pug to bow, "this is every bit as important as your work with the accounting ledgers. And you," she said to Pug, "should be grateful to me. I've rescued you from your lessons with Mr. Graveston for at least an hour. I'd hoped to recruit Millie as well, but Mrs. Harster has her busy in the conservatory."

Jack watched, reluctantly transfixed, as Ivy instructed Pug through the basic turns of a quadrille, explaining as she moved and laughingly pulling the confused boy into place when he turned the wrong way. Her smile lit up the room, he realized, and it was a fortunate man who would finally win her hand.

Suddenly feeling an inexplicable urge to learn the basic steps of the quadrille, he mentally shook himself with a sense of relief as Mary and Sophia entered the room, followed by Mr. Fuddleston, who looked none too happy to be there. Ivy paused in her instructions to Pug and smiled in genuine delight as she approached Sophia and Mary, both of whom she embraced with a laugh.

"Jack is behaving rather childishly about these lessons," she said to Sophia, who quirked a brow at her with a grin that spread as Ivy's face flushed. "Or rather, his Lordship," Ivy amended as Mary gracefully covered Ivy's discomfort with a gentle laugh of her own.

"He always was uncomfortable about such things," Mary said, laying a hand on his arm, and Jack wondered when his family's allegiance had turned from him to Ivy. He'd never even had the option for dancing lessons, and his mother well knew it. That she was evidently becoming more comfortable soothed his wounded pride, however, and he was more grateful than ever to Ivy for helping bring it about. She had explained her theory to him, that if Mary pretended in her new role it would eventually become natural, and it appeared she had the right of it.

Ivy seemed to have recovered her embarrassment at calling him "Jack" as she moved back out onto the floor and began telling the small group about her instructions with Pug. When she suggested they pair up, Sophia cast a glance in her brother's direction with a gleam in her eye he did not appreciate in the least.

"Oh, no," Sophia said to Ivy and moved toward Pug, whose expression suggested he was torn between mortification and delight, "I'll partner with Mr. Pug. You work with Jack, Ivy. He needs your expertise more than anyone. Mother and I know the basics, as does Mr. Fuddleston, I'm certain."

Mr. Fuddleston reddened considerably, and Jack noted with irritation that his solicitor seemed suddenly bashful. Such ridiculousness would ruin the best of men. Ivy looked at Sophia for a moment in apparent confusion before finally tipping her head in acquiescence and making her way to Jack's side. She smiled as she approached, and his breath hitched when she held out both hands to grasp his and pull him toward the center of the floor.

"Now," she said, "we are short one couple, so we will just have to do the best we can. I did ask Mrs. Harster and Watkins to join us, but they refused most adamantly."

Jack wished he could say that the next thirty minutes were painful and eternal, but in truth, the time passed altogether too quickly. Each turn had him anticipating the moment when he would again find himself at Ivy's side, and when he bumbled he was rewarded with her laughter, which sometimes had her doubled over. Mary and Sophia were equally delighted, and he found himself content for the first time in . . . well, perhaps ever.

"Now then," Ivy said, clasping her hands, her cheeks becomingly flushed, "we are also at liberty to dance the waltz, as Prinny has made it popular, but bear in mind, Sophia, that you and I are not to accept a waltz with the same gentleman more than three times at any one event."

Pug scrunched his nose. "Why?"

"Because it is tantamount to announcing a betrothal," Ivy told him, her eyes twinkling.

"Just because you dance with the same bloke three times in one night?" Pug looked as baffled as Jack often felt. "Seems awful strange."

Ivy winked at him. "Society is very strange. And not much to be done about it."

"So what is this 'waltz'?"

"Show him, Ivy," Sophia said, "and I will hum a minuet."

"Very well, Pug—come with me." Ivy led the poor boy to the middle of the ballroom, and Jack nearly snorted at Pug's horrified expression when Ivy placed his hand at her waist. Positioning her right hand in his, and laying her left upon his shoulder, she gave him a few basic instructions as Sophia began humming, tripping over herself in laughter as Ivy tried to teach the boy how to lead.

"One-two-three, one-two-three," Ivy chanted through her smiles as she pulled Pug along until, to Jack's amazement, the boy seemed to be catching the rhythm of the thing.

"He is actually doing it," Jack murmured to Fuddleston, who looked on with an expression Jack couldn't quite read. It was something akin to wistful, and when the little man noticed Jack's attention, he flushed.

"My mother taught me to waltz," he said with a shrug. "It was before most were doing it in England—it was considered too French, especially on the heels of the Revolution. Haven't had much opportunity to dance since then."

"Mama," Jack said, not quite believing he was saying it, "would you perhaps like to try your hand at the waltz with Mr. Fuddleston?"

Mary looked as stunned as he felt that he'd suggested it, but Fuddleston looked so forlorn, drat the man.

Fuddleston seemed to recover his wits better than any of the rest; he bowed to Mary and said, "Madam, it would be an honour."

Jack fought the lump in his throat when Clarence Fuddleston whisked his frail mother into a gentle waltz while Sophia kept up her humming of the minuet. It was idyllic and sweet, and he found his eyes burning with sentimental tears he had no time or use for. Clearing his throat, he tried to focus on the fact that Pug tripped repeatedly over his big feet, but that observation only led to the realization that when Ivy Carlisle laughed, Jack Elliot's heart thumped hard in his chest.

It was entirely too complicated, all of it, and for the millionth time he mentally cursed his dead grandfather up one side and down the other. Jack had no time to develop feelings for a young Society woman who was so beautifully charming and full of life it took his breath from his lungs. He was going to return to his life at sea, and entanglements on land were not an element he wanted to add to the complex mixture his reality had become. That he felt peace in such a domestic moment was the last thing he wanted. Sophia and Mary were in good hands with Lady Ivy, who would continue the friendship regardless of whom she married. There was no reason for him to remain in the thick of it; he was happier at sea. Of course he was.

The waltz finally came to a close as Sophia dramatically sang the last few notes of her impromptu accompaniment, and she turned to him, laughing. "Jack," his sister said, "it's your turn now. You must take a turn at the waltz with Lady Ivy."

Jack tightened his jaw but tried to smile. "I am feeling quite fatigued, actually. I believe I'll go lie down for a bit." He didn't want to look at Ivy but couldn't help meeting her gaze as he left the ballroom. She managed a tight smile of her own, but not before he glimpsed the unguarded flash of hurt that crossed her face.

It was for the best—she undoubtedly felt a sense of kinship with him because she had helped him when he'd been poisoned. That was something he had yet to thank her for, his conscience reminded him as he left the ballroom in long strides. Dismissing it with a shake of his head, he climbed the stairs to his room, not really feeling the need to rest. Ivy Carlisle didn't need him in her life any more than he needed her in his. Their arrangement was temporary and perfunctory. When his wretched training was finished, he would leave—and do so quickly. Fuddleston was more than capable of running the estate while Jack was away; everything was neat and tidy.

If he could have struck that final image of her hurt expression from his memory, he might have believed it.

Ivy sat in Jack's library and scribbled notes for her next column while she waited for Sophia to return home and gather the papers they needed to present to the city recorder. She tried not to think about the fact that the big oaf had hurt her feelings—she shouldn't care in the least that he didn't want to waltz with her. That she had managed to walk him through the steps of the quadrille was a miracle in itself.

Her quill scratched harder across the paper and she forced herself to relax and slow down so she would be able to make sense of her notes later on. She would have to write the column that evening and send it first thing in the morning to her editor; she had never been late turning in a piece before. She chastised herself for spending so much energy doing other things that she was now pressed for time.

A sound at the door caught her attention, and she spied Millie, the irreverent maid, beckoning to her. She stood as Millie looked over her shoulder down the hallway, and by the time Ivy reached her, Mrs. Harster had as well, and was giving the young woman orders to dust the parlor immediately as she had failed to do it earlier.

Millie opened her mouth with a glance at Ivy and then closed it, bobbing a quick curtsey.

"I'll walk with you to the parlor, Millie," Ivy said and accompanied the young woman to the room. Once inside, Millie turned to Ivy quickly, watching warily over her shoulder.

"Lady Ivy," she began, "I overheard Cook's assistant talking to someone out the back door last night. I was . . ." Millie blushed. "Well, never mind what I was doing. But he told the person that there would be other opportunities, that they must be patient."

Ivy frowned. "What do you suppose they were talking about?"

Millie's eyes grew round and large. "His Lordship, of course," she squeaked. "What else could it be? The man was all secret-like and looking over his shoulder. And then they argued but it got quiet, so I couldn't hear them and the man left."

"Who was the other man?"

Millie shrugged. "It was dark, and I couldn't see him."

Ivy paused and studied the young woman. "What were you doing outside, Millie?"

"I . . . I needed some fresh air."

"Were you with anyone else who also needed some fresh air?"

"There might have been someone I was going to meet and chat with, but he wasn't able to come. So I left and went home."

Ivy frowned. "Have a care, Millie. You do not always know whom you can trust and who would do you harm. Do you understand? Even if that someone is very handsome and charming."

Millie blushed. "How did you know, my lady?"

Ivy smiled, but as she thought of her sister, Caroline, it felt strained. "I know someone well, someone whose life was turned quite upside down by a handsome man, a man whose intentions were less than honourable."

Millie nodded soberly and chewed on her lip. "But ye'll remember what I said about Cook's assistant?"

"Yes, I will. What is his name?"

"Cook calls him 'Neddy.'"

Ivy left the young woman to her duties in the parlor and thoughtfully made her way back to the library. It would hardly do to start accusing the servants of nefarious deeds without more evidence than the word of a flighty housemaid. Still, it would bear thinking about.

She made her way back into the library, lost in thought, tapping the end of her quill against her lip. She was fully into the room before she realized Jack was at the desk, holding a sheaf of papers in his hand.

He had clearly been awaiting her return, and he quirked a brow at her and said, "This looks to be the first draft of an article, one that might be found in a ladies periodical?"

CHAPTER 20

Surprises can be delightful, and one should appreciate
those things that bring laughter into life.

Mistress Manners' Tips for Every-day Etiquette

I vy's heart thudded in her chest, and she stood frozen for a moment before feeling heat flood her face. She stormed across the room and grabbed at the papers, which Jack held just over her head.

"Give me those," she snapped and reached for them, but the odious man simply lifted them higher.

He smirked, and it made her blood boil. "That is my personal property," she bit out, "and you have no right to keep it from me."

"This is my house," he said, a maddening smile crossing his rugged features, "and I believe that entitles me to examine whatever I wish. And this is most interesting." He moved away from her then, neatly dodging her swipe as she jumped again to retrieve her notes.

"Lord Stansworth," she hissed and followed him as he crossed the room to the other side, taking another look at her papers.

"Mmm?" He shuffled the sheets, his expression going slack by the time he reached the last. "You're 'Mistress Manners'?" He stared at her then, and if she hadn't been so angry, his expression would have been priceless.

"No. They're . . . they're Nana's. She is Mistress Manners. And please be decent and keep her secret."

"But this is your script. I would know your handwriting anywhere from the infernal notes you constantly give me on how to 'comport' myself."

Ivy took a deep breath and briefly closed her eyes. "I make notes for her on occasion," she said lamely and held his gaze for a moment before finally dropping her eyes and massaging her temples.

"You do not lie well, Ivy."

"I know that! Just give me my notes, Jack."

"Why?"

She glared at him. "Because I need them!"

"No. Why would you keep it a secret?"

Ivy sputtered for a moment before pulling her thoughts together. "Because it is unseemly!"

Jack shook his head at her, the papers still firmly in his hands. "Unseemly to write about good manners?"

Ivy turned her attention to the window and slowly walked toward it. "I receive money for it," she muttered.

"I'm sorry?" She heard him approach and felt him close behind her as he brushed against her sleeve.

"It is a paid position," she said. "And I need to remain anonymous to prevent any embarrassment to my family."

"Ivy," he said, and she finally turned to look up at him. "There is no shame in this."

"My family is aristocracy," she murmured, suddenly feeling tears burning in her eyes and not knowing why. "It is not done, my lord."

He palmed her cheek with his hand, an oddly tender expression crossing his face. "This is a rule that can be broken, my lady. Your family should feel pride, not shame. You are very witty, in fact. It pains me to admit it, but I find this article very entertaining."

"You do?" She heard the hopeful note in her voice and found it rather pathetic. But he was standing so very close to her, and touching her cheek, and suddenly nothing else seemed very important.

"I do. I believe you are a very talented writer."

Ivy's breath hitched as he lowered his head and slowly touched his lips to hers, just the lightest of contact at first, and then more urgent as he moved his hand to the back of her neck. She suddenly understood why Caroline was willing to throw caution to the wind and run away with her handsome soldier. Moving closer to him, she sighed as Jack encircled her in his arms and pulled her up against him. She gripped his lapels and felt she was drowning when he broke the contact and pushed her gently back, holding her at arm's length with her papers still in his hand.

Ivy blinked, making an effort to focus on him and the expression on his face that showed as much bafflement as she felt. His breath came rapidly, and he stared at her for a long, silent moment before slowly releasing her arms.

"Best not to include that in your article," he whispered and handed her the notes, which she took with numb fingers. "I'll keep your secret."

Stunned, she watched him leave the room in long strides and heard the front door slam moments later. It was some time before she realized she hadn't told him what she'd learned from Millie.

Ivy rather wished she hadn't accepted the invitation for the Barringtons' soiree later that evening on behalf of the Elliots and herself. If she could only have a bit more time to process what had happened between her and Jack, she might be able to pretend it had never happened, even if he was in her presence. As it was, the soiree was that evening, and she had no choice but to put on a brave face and attend.

Giving her mother a perfunctory good-bye as she left the house and climbed into the carriage, Ivy stewed on the ride to meet Mary and Sophia. The earl's carriage picked the women up at his mother's house, and when Ivy was settled in across from Jack, she found herself unable to look him in the eye. She would have been delighted to lay blame for the kiss entirely at his feet, but she knew she had been a willing participant.

It was unfamiliar territory for her; other than the fact that propriety certainly frowned on such actions, she was at a loss to explain why it had even happened, or why she had enjoyed it so very much. No other man of her acquaintance had so much as turned her head in recent years, and she had accepted the fact that she would ultimately find herself in a loveless marriage that she hoped would at least be amicable.

But this? The kiss had been delicious. And to try to forget it was the best course of action, not only for herself but for Jack. He had his share of entanglements with his new life—the last thing he needed was amorous attention from his mentor.

No. Tonight she would throw herself into the task of finding Jack a suitable match. She would observe and consider several eligible options over the next few weeks of Society rounds. She would find the perfect girl for him. The thought of him kissing another woman the way he'd kissed her made her face flush and her stomach feel funny, but she decided to dismiss it.

She didn't so much as glance at Jack throughout the carriage ride, so she couldn't say if he was ignoring her as well. The ride to the Barringtons' was mercifully short, and if Mary noticed anything amiss, she covered it well with light conversation in which only Sophia bothered to engage.

"I have found a good prospect for our girls' home, Ivy," Sophia said as the carriage pulled to a stop alongside the house. Ivy looked at Sophia, who was eyeing her with suspicion. Sophia was too perceptive by half—of course she would sense the tension inside the conveyance.

"I'm so glad to hear it." Ivy attempted to shake her discontent as she took the footman's hand and stepped out of the carriage. When Sophia joined her, Ivy linked arms. "When shall we examine it?"

"The owner told me to expect to see it next week. I do think it sounds promising, although I've only ever seen it from the outside."

As they approached the Barringtons' front door, Sophia tipped her head toward Ivy's and lowered her voice. "What was the meaning of that awkwardness?"

Ivy shrugged and tried for a light tone. "It was nothing, really. Just an exchange of words with your brother earlier today." *Words and more,* Ivy thought, but it wasn't the time or place to take Sophia into her confidence.

A quick glance over her shoulder showed Jack and Mary approaching, and her breath caught in her throat for a moment at the sight of Jack the Rowdy Sailor in his evening best. If he didn't turn the eyes of Society misses, he would certainly catch the attention of the married women who were often on the prowl for new lovers.

The latter thought made Ivy even more irritated than the first, and she looked forward again, pasting a smile on her face and handing their invitation to the butler. She could not care less where Jack's future lay; her only worry was to see that he become socially acceptable.

Once proper introductions were made, Lady Barrington paired those present and they entered the ballroom by rank. As luck would have it, the good lady paired Ivy with Jack. Ivy forced another smile, placed her hand on Jack's arm, and stared straight ahead.

"Lovely weather this evening, wouldn't you say, Lady Ivy?"

Ivy glanced up at Jack's face, barely keeping her mouth from dropping open. His accent was flawless, and he sounded as though he'd lived amongst upper-crust Society his entire life.

"Yes, indeed it is, my lord," Ivy answered, shoving down a sense of irritation. All of the times she had told him to soften a bit of his piratical demeanor! He spoke like an earl, carried himself with a great degree of majesty, and, if it weren't for the slightest of smirks that fleetingly crossed his features, she might have believed the sailor talk had been an act.

"I do hope we see the sun again tomorrow," he continued as they made their way into the dining room. He held her seat out and gently scooted her in, then sat next to her with a smile. "I should very much like a nice ride through the park."

"You must find yourself more comfortable on your stallion these days, then," Ivy said.

"I should say so," Jack said and leaned back slightly in his chair as a servant placed the first course before him. "Why, I cannot think of anything I'd rather do than ride around town on a horse. It is the pleasantest of pastimes."

Ivy did her best to keep her eyes from rolling back into her head. Lord Sticklemore smiled at Jack from across the table. "I do agree, Stansworth. Nice to make the acquaintance of a fellow horse enthusiast."

"His Lordship is full of surprises." Ivy stabbed her fork into her salad. She could feel Jack's gaze on her, and she looked up to see his lips twitch. The brows he raised gave the impression of complete innocence, however, and Ivy found herself in the unusual position of forcing herself to behave.

"Lord Hovley," Ivy said to the young, blonde gentleman seated next to her, "how is your sister faring? This is her first Season, if I'm not much mistaken."

Lord Arthur Hovley, the Duke of Sommershire, smiled and nodded. He was a friendly sort, and Ivy had danced with him on more than one occasion. As much as her parents would have approved of a match with him, however, she could never bring herself to see him as more than a brother.

"She is doing well, thank you. Enjoying her coming out most ardently," Lord Hovley told her. "And she is most looking forward to seeing you again."

"I don't believe I've had the pleasure," Jack said over Ivy's shoulder.

"Oh, yes. Your grace, may I present John Elliot, the Earl of Stansworth. My lord, his grace Arthur Hovley, the Duke of Sommershire."

Lord Hovley inclined his head with a smile, and Ivy glanced at Jack, who had suddenly sat up much straighter in his chair and seemed . . . bigger. She frowned a bit and turned her attention back to Lord Hovley. "Please extend my greetings to Lady Jacqueline," she said to him. "And when I next host tea, I shall extend an invitation well in advance so she might plan accordingly. I suspect her days are quite full."

"Indeed, indeed. And my mother is most anxious that she make a good match without much delay, as my second sister will have her Season next year."

Ivy understood completely. The oldest sister was to be married first before the others would be allowed, which had become part of the problem with Ivy's own circumstances. She was the second daughter, and sister to a woman who had cast reason aside and ruined everything.

Ivy smiled. "I am certain Lady Jacqueline will do splendidly. She is a beautiful girl, and much accomplished."

Ivy glanced past Lord Hovley and down the table to where Sophia sat, a pleasant expression on her face despite her placement between one very loud, aging dowager duchess and one short, portly viscount who had already outlived two wives.

Ivy didn't worry so much for Sophia. She had worked with the upper classes most of her life and knew how to behave, even if it was all an act. She did worry about Mary—she didn't want the woman bullied by some of Society's meaner matrons and was glad to see her seated between two gentlemen whose prowess or egos were dampened by their dullish personalities. They spoke to Mary most kindly, it seemed to Ivy as she observed their demeanor, and Mary smiled and responded in her gentle tones.

Jack, on the other hand. Jack. She glanced at him, irritated that he had played so incredibly dim-witted on occasion and allowed her to fear that he would never learn to pass himself off as a gentleman.

She ought to be grateful, she supposed, that he had the wherewithal to accomplish it.

The rest of the meal was consumed with idle, pleasant chit-chat, with some politics thrown in for good measure among the gentlemen. The ladies then retired to the drawing room while the gentlemen enjoyed a glass of port.

Mary was swallowed in a group of women, most of whom Ivy felt were kind, and they sat with her at the hearth. Sophia pounced on Ivy as soon as she entered and drew her to a corner for privacy while the other women in the group talked about their children and amazing prospects for their futures.

"I'll not wait another minute. Tell me what is happening with you!" Sophia whispered.

Ivy sighed. There were a million possible ways to explain to Sophia exactly what had happened earlier, but after mulling it over for a moment, she opted for bluntness.

"Your brother kissed me in the library."

Sophia's mouth dropped open, and she lifted her hand to cover it. "He did what? He wouldn't even waltz with you this morning!"

Ivy winced. "Well, there it is. I am not about to let it happen again, and I think he rather regrets it himself."

Sophia watched her for a moment with her gaze that seemed to see into the soul. She was bright and practical, and Ivy fought the need to fidget under her friend's regard. "*Can* you forget it, then? Because you still have a fair amount of time to spend time with him."

Ivy straightened her shoulders. How had she let them droop? Perhaps her spent emotional energy had sapped her strength. "Of course I can forget it. It was an unconscionable mistake that could very well have ruined me!"

Sophia nodded once. "Good. I certainly have no objection to your having affection for my brother, but the timing is awfully bad."

"I know this." Ivy glared at Sophia.

Sophia shrugged, eyes wide. "I'm protecting you from yourself."

"I do not need protecting," Ivy ground out and glanced around to be sure nobody had overheard their conversation. She needn't have worried; the other ladies in attendance were still discussing their precious offspring, bragging largely to Mary, as she was a fresh audience who had yet to hear all of the stories.

Lady Barrington beckoned to the two young women, and they made their way across the room to her. She was a handsome woman, aging well, and Ivy had always liked her. When they reached her, she began a lively conversation about new fashions and the most desirable balls for which one hoped to receive an invitation. Sophia complimented her on the wonderful dinner they had just enjoyed.

Lady Barrington beamed, and, as irritated with Sophia as Ivy was, she found herself proud of her new friend. She was smart, and she would be just fine. Ivy had deliberately chosen this particular event to attend because she'd had a sneaking suspicion that she and Sophia might well be the youngest people present. She wanted to ease Sophia into testing the waters before sending her to the sharks at bigger gatherings: female sharks who were going to hate her for her beauty and resent her for her recent good fortune. Never mind that it should have been hers all along.

A short time later, they left and met up with the men in the conservatory so that Lady Barrington might impress them all with her abilities at the pianoforte. Ivy wasn't entirely certain how it had happened, but she found herself separated from Sophia and Mary and sandwiched again between Jack and Lord Hovley. She wanted to ignore Jack completely, but Sophia's words rang in Ivy's head, and she determined to be adult and practical.

Besides which, his thigh was nestled intimately against hers. Any hope for ignoring him flew out the window.

"I do hope you enjoyed your glass of port, my lord," she said to Jack and bared her teeth in what she hoped looked like a smile.

"You are speaking to me, then?" he murmured.

"Of course. Why would you imagine otherwise?"

His lips quirked in a smile, and she had the distinct impression she was being mocked. "So that is how we shall play it."

Ivy flushed and clenched her teeth together, staring straight ahead. He shifted in the seat and pressed his leg even closer. She wouldn't have thought it possible. The strains of Lady Barrington's pianoforte sounded in the room, and Ivy jumped a bit in surprise.

Jack chuckled and she elbowed him discreetly. He leaned in close to her ear and whispered, "I didn't have port. Lord Barrington keeps a stash of whiskey hidden in the library where his wife will never find it."

Against her will and better judgment, she felt a laugh bubbling up and bit the insides of her cheeks to keep it from escaping. Perhaps Jack might find himself some kindred spirits among the *ton* after all.

One musical number turned into two, which melted into three, after which Lord Barrington stood to recite a few original pieces of poetry, which were largely nonsensical and dramatic. Ivy clapped politely when their hosts finished their entertainment and would have found it utterly impossible to repeat with any clarity the things she'd heard.

Ivy smiled at something Lord Hovley said to her, although she wasn't entirely certain what it was. What was wrong with her? A perfectly nice gentleman, a kind friend, and she couldn't even focus enough to manage one little conversation with the man?

The problem was that Jack was everywhere—he was brazen beyond words with his leg pressed against hers, and his very scent enveloped her senses. It was so incredibly pleasant, and she would have laughed if someone had told her she would one day come to appreciate the smell of a man. A *smell*, for heaven's sake. It was soap, freshly laundered clothing, and an elusive something that was uniquely his. Lord Hovley had no discernible smell.

She told herself to jump up from the chair but found herself oddly rooted to it. Jack leaned in close once again and said, "I do believe the carriage awaits us outside. Were you planning to remain here all night long?"

"No, I was not," she snapped and stood. The sudden absence of his body heat was unmistakable and disconcerting. "And you, sir," she added in a brusque whisper, "are to rise when a lady does."

"You are flustered, Lady Ivy," Jack told her as he stood, and she almost wished she had left him sitting in the chair. He was tall, and she felt infinitely less powerful with him looming over her.

She drew a deep breath and briefly closed her eyes. "I am well in control, my lord," she said evenly.

His grin suggested he believed otherwise, but he had sense enough to refrain from comment. "You'd best take care, Lady Ivy," he said in those measured, aristocratic tones, "or you might find yourself behaving contrary to Mistress Manners' advice. I do believe that woman has written a piece or two about keeping one's temper, especially in public. Wouldn't do to cause a scene."

He offered her his arm, and she very nearly turned away from it when she saw Lady Barrington out of the corner of her eye. If Ivy were to cut Jack, her whole purpose in tutoring him would be moot. She linked her hand through the crook of his arm and smiled up at him. "Amazing how well you seem to be speaking today," she murmured. "Your pronunciation is absolutely impeccable. Perhaps the poison knocked your tongue loose."

"I have you to thank for my improvements, Lady Ivy."

"That is a barefaced lie, and you and I both know it." She urged him toward the door, and they exited to find Sophia and Mary donning wraps and awaiting them. "And furthermore," she said as the butler retrieved her cloak, "your lessons are about to triple."

CHAPTER 21

*To see a friend hurt can be one of life's most painful experiences;
one must remain calm in the face of distress.*

Mistress Manners' Tips for Every-day Etiquette

Jack made his way to the stables the next morning, running a hand through his hair and realizing belatedly that he'd neglected to grab his hat. What did it matter? He was an earl. Perhaps he would set a new trend.

His growing attraction for Lady Ivy Carlisle was reaching uncomfortable levels, and he wondered if he was about to be caught in a snare of his own making. While he had begun toying with some gentle flirting and teasing, he was finding that it was becoming less about teasing her, and more about feeling very real.

He waited while his new stable master saddled his stallion and led the horse out; then he swung his leg up and over the mount, grateful if nothing else for Ivy's insistence that he become more practiced on horseback; hopefully it would allow him to get away from thoughts of her, if only momentarily.

He guided the horse through the streets to the park, where he bypassed the congested paths in favor of the more secluded wooded and grassy areas. There he allowed the big stallion to take the lead and run despite the fact that such was not technically allowed in the park. He welcomed the rush of cold wind and rain against his face, feeling freer than he had since that first fateful night Clarence Fuddleston had entered his well-ordered life.

Leaning forward in the stirrups, he urged the horse faster, wishing he could guide the beast to the ends of the earth and keep riding even from there. He had had no business kissing Lady Ivy Carlisle, none at all. The feel of her in his arms had been utter perfection, though, and he admitted to himself that he had wanted to kiss her from the moment she'd boarded the ship and demanded he return with her to his dying grandfather's bedside. If only she hadn't looked at him with those blasted luminous eyes, hurting because she knew her family wouldn't welcome news of her "career," he never would have been so foolish. He had tried to resume his friendly banter with her at the soiree but her nearness had driven him nearly to distraction. Of course, he had pushed the bounds of propriety to their limits and beyond by sitting so close to her. He supposed he had thought to shock her, but found he had instead become caught in his own trap.

If only he hadn't felt the stirrings of mad jealousy when she had smiled and laughed at dinner with her "dear friend," the blond paragon of dukely perfection, he might have been thinking a little more clearly. He had nobody to blame but himself. It certainly wasn't her fault that she was completely unaware of her own allure. And even if she had been aware, she still wouldn't have been responsible for his reaction to seeing her conversing on a casual level with another man.

That was the worst of it, he supposed. He wanted someone else to blame. But lately he had been thinking less of his career on the high seas and more about anticipating his lovely mentor's next visit.

Closing his eyes against the stinging rain that now fell hard and fast even through the trees, he pulled slightly on the reins and sat up straight, settling back into the saddle to allow the horse to cool a bit. He caught his breath as the horse jerked wildly to the right, and as Jack shifted his weight again, the animal screamed and reared up. Jack clamped his legs tightly around the horse and tried to utter a command that would calm the animal, but after slashing at the air with its front legs, the stallion slammed to the ground hard and then reared up again, twisting wildly and throwing Jack from his back.

He hit the ground hard, seeing stars as his head made contact with the earth. The last thing he registered before the world faded to black was the fact that his booted foot was still stuck in the stirrup as the stallion thrashed yet again.

Ivy paced the confines of her bedroom, wanting desperately to talk to someone yet not wanting to be around anyone at all. She could go to Nana, she supposed, but how to tell her that the Earl of Stansworth had kissed her most thoroughly in the library, where anyone could have seen them—and she had most thoroughly enjoyed it. Every moment of it. And then he had sat scandalously close to her at the soiree, and she had wanted to climb right into his lap and thread her fingers through that silky black hair.

Her mother was out to tea, and her father was likely at Tattersalls. Perhaps if things had been different between Ivy and her mother, she might have appreciated her as a confidante. Yet even if Caroline hadn't ruined any chance of talking with her mother about illicit kisses in libraries, their relationship had never been one to accommodate such familiarity.

Ivy needed to collect herself in a hurry because she was due to meet with Sophia in thirty minutes to tour a building that would possibly suit their needs for the girls' school. She called herself a fool a million times over for reliving the kiss repeatedly and told herself to think of something serious.

A frantic banging on the front door pulled Ivy from her thoughts, and she frowned, leaving her bedroom and peering over the front landing as Farrell, the butler, opened the door.

Pug stood on the other side, white as a sheet and soaking wet from the rain, his eyes wide and terrified. Ivy dashed down the front stairs as Farrell was preparing to close the door on the boy, disgust clearly stamped across his lofty features.

"What is it?" Ivy asked, shouldering her way past Farrell and pulling Pug into the house.

"Accident in the park," the boy told her, a tear escaping his eye and rolling down his cheek. He wiped at his eye impatiently and scowled. "Master Jack got thrown from his horse."

Ivy's heart thudded hard in her chest. "Where is he?"

"Constable in the park saw the horse throw 'im, brought 'im home." Pug clenched his hands together. "'E's awful bad, Miss. Face is a mess, an' 'e won't wake up."

"Please get my wrap, Farrell, and have the coach brought around," Ivy said and turned back to Pug. "Has the doctor been summoned? And Sophia?"

"Doctor is on 'is way, an' I came to you first." The boy shrugged miserably. "Didn't know what to do."

Farrell helped Ivy into her cloak, and when the coach pulled up in front, Ivy took Pug by the arm and led him out to it. The ride to the earl's town home was silent, and Ivy began to feel sick from the knot of fear that sat like a stone in her stomach. She needed to get word to Sophia and Mary, but she would assess the situation herself first. Sophia would not appreciate being sheltered, but Ivy was unwilling to alert Mary yet, to burden her with questions but no answers.

The walk to the front door, past a serious Watkins, and then up the stairs to Jack's suite seemed to take an eternity. Ivy's feet felt leaden, and the more she tried to hurry, the more she feared she would never reach him. Tossing her cloak off when she reached the dressing room, she entered the earl's bedroom breathless and very much afraid.

Clarence Fuddleston and Lord Anthony Blake stood at the bed, and Blake had a towel at Jack's head, gingerly working at it. Ivy grew dizzy as she neared the bed and saw that the towel was liberally stained with dark red patches, and she clutched the large foot post. She couldn't see Jack's face, as Blake had it obscured by the cloth.

She looked at Fuddleston with wide eyes. "What has happened?" she asked him, her voice barely escaping the knot in her throat.

Fuddleston was as pale as Pug. "The stable master examined the stallion, found him bloodied from a small nail wedged into the saddle. The man swears he didn't see it when he put it on the animal. Possible, I suppose, if it was angled just right. If his Lordship was riding forward when he left and then settled back into the saddle later at the park . . ."

Blake held the towel at the back of Jack's head, his jaw clenched. "I need another cloth," he barked and glanced up at Pug, who ran to the doorway where Mrs. Harster, looking faint, stood with fresh towels and a basin of water. Blake dropped the bloodied towel to the floor in a heap and grabbed the fresh one Pug handed him.

Ivy's stomach turned and she felt decidedly nauseated when she got a good look at Jack's face before Anthony Blake covered it again with the towel. Ivy wasn't sure how he even knew where to dab; Jack's face was a red mess and she was glad he was, for the moment, unconscious.

"Lady Ivy, perhaps you might be more comfortable in the dressing room," Fuddleston said to her gently.

Ivy swallowed and shook her head. Thinking of Nana's steely resolve and utter disregard for Society's good opinion, she removed her shawl and laid it across a narrow bench at the foot of the bed. "I am here to help," she said and unbuttoned her cuffs, rolling back her sleeves. "What shall I do?" she asked Blake.

Blake glanced at her, his face grim. "Until the doctor arrives, I'm not entirely certain. I do know we need to stop the bleeding. Perhaps you might hold the cloth here while I place another behind his head. Fuddleston, perhaps you should go question the staff, particularly the outside servants, about whether they have seen anyone lurking around the stables. You have Lord Stansworth's ear these days more than anyone, and it falls to you to discover what is happening in this household."

Fuddleston nodded and turned to Mrs. Harster as he retrieved his suit coat from the floor where he must have flung it. "You remain here, then, to fetch anything his Lordship might require," he told the woman, who nodded faintly.

Ivy tried to reach Jack from Blake's side but found the bed too tall and Blake too broad. She frowned and crossed to the opposite side of the massive bed, where she made use of the step stool and then crawled awkwardly across the expanse of mattress. Blake stared at her for a moment before raising a brow and the corner of his mouth. Whatever he was thinking, he kept it to himself, but Ivy couldn't help but blush.

"I do hope you're not one for gossip, my lord," she said to Blake as she situated herself near Jack's shoulders and gingerly took the edge of the towel.

"Wouldn't dream of it, my lady," Blake told her and glanced at Mrs. Harster over his shoulder. "More towels, if you please, and find that cursed doctor!"

The housekeeper scurried from the room with wide eyes, likely grateful to have a purpose.

Jack's poor face was battered, and Ivy cringed as she began wiping away at the worst of the blood covering his cheeks and forehead. "I need a bit of water," she murmured as Anthony Blake situated the bulk of the towel behind Jack's head. The metallic smell of blood very nearly overwhelmed her, and Ivy swallowed hard, her mouth dry.

Blake reached for the basin of water that Mrs. Harster had carried into the room; he held it above Jack's chest as Ivy dipped the corner of the towel into it. Wringing it out, she winced at the pink tinge the water had taken on and bit her lip as she again plied herself to the task of determining the extent of the wounds on Jack's face.

The very fact that he was so very still as she cleared the smears and patches of blood had her blinking back burning tears. Nana would definitely not cry, she reminded herself as she cleared her throat and decided to pretend she was a nurse. What was a little blood, after all? And he would be fine—of course he would. No need for emotional outbursts or fits of sadness.

Blake gingerly put a thumb to Jack's eyelid and lifted it to reveal the staring, but thankfully intact, tawny-colored eye. "Looks as though his brow took the worst of it," he murmured as blood pooled around Jack's eyebrow. Blake hastily moved his thumb and pulled at the towel, applying pressure to the gash. Ivy felt light-headed and her arms tingled; it took every ounce of Nana-channeling she could manage to keep from tipping over on the bed herself.

Ivy continued to clear the smudges around the earl's chin and cheek while Blake held the cloth in place over the cut on the brow. "What is happening here, my lord?" she said, looking up at Blake. He stood very close, and Ivy registered the fact that her mother would have an apoplectic fit if she could see her daughter perched atop one earl's bed, inches from another. Suddenly all of the world's rules and regulations meant little as she wondered what sort of danger was afoot in Jack Elliot's house.

Blake's flat, almost angry expression was at odds with the one he usually showed the public. The mocking, arrogant, jaded lord seemed to have been left at the door, and in his place stood a man very concerned for the welfare of a friend. "Someone wants him dead," Blake told her. "He is going to need a guard by his side all hours of the day and night."

Ivy smiled a bit. "He will hate that."

"Yes, he will." Blake studied her for a moment, and Ivy found herself hard-pressed to maintain his direct gaze. "What is he to you, then?" Blake asked her.

"I am helping him and his family ease their way into Society."

"And lying to yourself."

Ivy blinked at the bluntness. "I'm sure I do not know what you mean, my lord," she said stiffly.

"We are close enough associates by this point, Lady Ivy, to

dispense with formalities. You will please call me Anthony—we did share a dance once, after all."

Ivy's lips quirked despite her mounting fear for the man whose face she held in her hands. "One dance, my lord, and that was under duress. Proper young ladies do not do well to be seen overlong in the company of rakes and rogues."

"You wound me, Ivy." Blake lifted Jack's head slightly and pulled the towel from the pillow, substituting a fresh one.

Ivy swallowed again at the sight of the spent cloth that dropped to the floor with a sickening *thunk*. "He's losing too much blood." Her heart climbed into her throat. An alarming thought forced its way into her consciousness and she glanced at the empty doorway to be sure the doctor hadn't yet arrived. "We must not let Dr. Featherstone bleed him with leeches. Jack was most adamant about it the last time."

Blake frowned as he loosened Jack's cravat and opened the topmost buttons on the once white shirt. "He has had some kind of bad experience with leeches?" he said.

"I do not know, but it stands to reason, with him losing so much blood, it hardly makes sense to take even more from him. It isn't as though he has poison in his system this time."

Blake glanced up at her. "It does stand to reason. And—"

"What is happening? Ivy, we had an appointment, and then I receive word that there has been an accident?" The demand came from the doorway; Ivy looked over her shoulder to see Sophia standing there looking a mixture of fear and fury. "Why did you not send for me immediately?"

Sophia entered the room, shedding her outer garments as she approached the far side of the bed and climbed up next to Ivy. To her credit, she gentled her approach as she looked at her brother lying still under Ivy's and Blake's hands.

"I didn't want your mother to worry until we knew . . . well, until we know how bad it is," Ivy told her, her heart twisting at the anguished look on Sophia's face. Ivy frowned and reached for Sophia's shoulder, pulling back at the last moment to keep from bloodying her friend's dress. "The doctor is on his way."

"Jack," Sophia whispered and placed her hand atop his head. "Please."

Ivy glanced at Blake for help with a reassuring word or kind response and was exasperated to find him staring at Sophia, mouth agape. It was likely he'd never before seen Jack's beautiful sister—he had yet to meet her at any official functions.

With a roll of her eyes, she turned her attention back to Sophia, who by now seemed to realize there was another in the room.

"Who are you?" she demanded as she looked up at Blake.

He closed his mouth as Ivy gestured to him. "Miss Sophia Elliot, may I introduce Lord Anthony Blake, heir to the Earl of Wilshire."

"And how do you know my brother?" Sophia asked Blake, who continued to regard her without so much as blinking.

"We are friends," Blake finally said. "And it is a pleasure to meet you."

Ivy considered the absurdity of the introduction as they were gathered there around a gravely wounded man, two of them smeared in blood up to their elbows.

Sophia turned her attention back to Ivy. "What happened; do you know?"

Ivy quietly relayed what little they had learned from Fuddleston, wishing she could shield Sophia from the truth.

"Who is trying to kill my brother?" Sophia looked at Ivy with eyes that filmed over. "I don't understand."

"We will find the culprit," Ivy told her, hoping they would before the killer met with success.

"You should know, Lord Blake, that if you are in any way connected with the troubles Jack is experiencing, I will hunt you down myself." Sophia's tone was pleasant enough, but Ivy briefly closed her eyes. Sophia's Season would not go at all well if she threatened members of the upper class.

Ivy motioned for Sophia to hold the end of the towel while Ivy reached for Jack's hand and put her fingers at his wrist. His pulse was constant, thank heaven, and, a little sigh escaping her lips, Ivy held out hope that Jack Elliot might be strong enough to survive just about anything. One thing was certain—he was definitely thick-headed enough.

CHAPTER 22

Comfort often comes from those whom we
may not have realized are our friends.
Mistress Manners' Tips for Every-day Etiquette

I vy eyed the doctor warily as he entered Jack's bedchamber with his black medicine bag, wondering if the man had secured the fresh leeches he had mentioned last time. She glanced at Anthony Blake, whose face remained impassive, but she noticed a further tightening of his jaw.

"Took your time, man," Blake said to Doctor Featherstone. "He's nearly bled to death waiting for you."

Doctor Featherstone shot Blake a flat look and doffed his coat and gloves. Rolling up his sleeves, he shouldered Blake out of the way and gave a quick glance to the two young women kneeling on the bed.

"You mustn't bleed him," Ivy blurted out. "He's lost too much already."

Featherstone didn't bother to look at her, but carefully turned

Jack's head to the side and bent close to examine the back of it. "I've yet to even fully see the extent of the injuries, my lady. I will make that determination when I have a better understanding of his Lordship's condition."

"You'll not bleed him." Blake's face was stony and impassive, and standing there as he was, hands on hips, his white shirt smeared with blood, he looked fearsome. Ivy would certainly not want to argue with him in such a state, and apparently he had given Doctor Featherstone enough pause that he glanced at the earl before continuing to probe. He replaced the towel at the back of Jack's head.

"We must immediately stitch," the doctor said as he looked closely at the worst of the offending cuts on Jack's face, across his eyebrow and down onto his nose. He looked over his shoulder again at Blake. "You will help me," he said, and then he looked at Ivy and Sophia. "You two will leave."

"I am staying right here," Sophia told the man, "and we do not have time to waste arguing about it."

Ivy wasn't sure she had the stomach to watch the doctor string thread through Jack's face, so it was just as well she had been ordered from the room.

"I am going downstairs to speak with Mr. Fuddleston," she said and laid a hand on Sophia's arm. "Send for me if you need me."

Sophia nodded, and Ivy crawled across the mattress and slid to the floor trying without success to keep the bedding free of bloody handprints. As she looked back again at Jack, her breath caught in her throat and her eyes began to burn. He was so frighteningly still. Worst of all was the fact that she had been so horribly short to him the night before. She would take it all back in a heartbeat. It hardly mattered that he had been teasing her all along, that he had allowed her to believe he was incapable of playing the part she was training him for. Perhaps he had hoped his impeccable speech and manners would be a pleasant surprise for her.

Thinking along those lines was even worse, and she closed her eyes as she hurried from the room, tears escaping and making their way down her face. Wiping impatiently at the tears with the backs of her hands, she walked down the second-floor hallway to the front staircase and descended to the foyer. The butler was in the process of closing the parlor doors when Ivy approached him.

"Is Mr. Fuddleston inside?"

"Yes, my lady."

"I must speak with him."

Watkins opened the doors again, and she entered to find Clarence Fuddleston sitting near the hearth. He stood immediately at her entrance, eyes widened at her appearance.

Fuddleston moved out of the way and indicated for her to take the seat he had been occupying. She sank into it gratefully, and he pulled another chair close to the hearth so the two of them might converse. Now that she had a moment to sit and think, Ivy felt positively shaky, and the tears gathered again.

"What news, then?" Fuddleston asked her, his serious eyes round and blinking behind his spectacles.

She shrugged, miserable. "The doctor is going to stitch the worst of the wounds. Lord Blake and Miss Elliot are going to assist him. And then, I suppose, we wait." Another tear streaked down her cheek and she wiped at it, embarrassed.

Fuddleston handed her a clean, folded handkerchief from his inside coat pocket and gave her a slight nod. "I have been speaking with members of the staff, and nobody recognized anything out of the ordinary. No new maids or other servants hired within the last few weeks, other than the stable master."

"Yesterday I spoke with one of the scullery maids, Millie," Ivy told him, wiping delicately at her nose and wishing she were alone so she could blow it. She relayed the conversation between the cook's assistant and the mysterious stranger in the back gardens.

"I will speak with her right away," he said. "And as for the immediate future, perhaps the family should consider taking his Lordship to the country estate. We might see a lessening of these attacks if he is no longer in the city. The estate is south, on the coast, good healing air," Fuddleston mused. "I shall propose it to Mrs. Elliot and Miss Elliot as soon as possible. Give him a day or two to heal a bit before we move him."

Ivy's heart thudded in her chest, first because she hoped desperately Jack would live and be able to be moved, and second because the Elliots would be miles away from London and she would miss them dreadfully.

Clarence Fuddleston took his leave, and Ivy sat alone in the parlor, sick to her stomach and so consumed with fear and worry she thought she would certainly choke on it. It would hardly do her any good to sit and stew, but she was at a loss to formulate a plan that included herself being useful.

She slowly climbed back up the stairs and took a seat in Jack's dressing room, not daring to venture back into the bedchamber. It really was a sound idea to take Jack far away from London. She somehow couldn't bear the thought and was frustrated with herself. But truth be told, she hadn't finished her tutoring sessions with him or Sophia and Mary, and she really should accompany them to the country to complete the task properly. She could come along formally as the women's guest, or perhaps she could twist Nana's arm into accompanying her as a chaperone.

Yes, that would be the best answer for everything, Ivy simply had to travel with the Elliots. Jack would require extra time to heal. That would be fine, though. It would all be fine if he would just awaken.

Fuddleston entered the dressing room and took a seat next to her, his face grave as ever. "Lady Ivy," he said, "Cook's assistant seems to have disappeared without notice. I think it safe to assume that he was at least partially responsible for these attempts on his Lordship's life, though almost certainly not the instigating party."

Ivy nodded, swallowing. Everything was suddenly so much more real. Before, she had almost been able to convince herself that Jack's two accidents were merely that. Coincidental. Plain bad luck. She would have to face the fact that someone clearly wanted the new earl dead and wasn't planning to stop until he achieved that end.

"I do think it a wise idea to take him out of the city," Ivy said quietly. "I believe that ultimately the decision should be left to his mother and Sophia; I will discuss it with Sophia in a moment."

He smiled at her then, and she knew he was viewing her with empathy. "Would you like me to retrieve Miss Elliot for you?"

Ivy smiled back, weakly, but a smile nonetheless. "Thank you for the offer, but I ought to venture back in there. I want to support Sophia and see . . . see . . ." She swallowed hard. "See how his Lordship fares."

He nodded. "I shall take your leave, then. I will ask the doctor's assessment of the earl's condition, and then I must continue my inquiries."

"Very good. And thank you, Mr. Fuddleston."

He smiled at her and rose, entering the bedchamber quietly. Ivy wished more than anything that she could stay in the dressing room forever and deny that there were bad people in the world who intentionally sought the harm of others. It was ever so much lovelier to mentally reside in a place where people all sought the good of one another. And while she had to admit that even within the walls of her own home things were not perfect, there was no overt hostility, and she was accustomed to tranquillity. To a world where people followed the rules.

Fuddleston exited the bedchamber a moment later and approached Ivy, taking her limp hand in both of his. "The doctor believes he will be well, my lady. His good health and vigor are to his advantage in the healing process."

She felt the lump form in her throat again and nodded at the man, touched that he would have a care for her state of mind, regardless of the fact that no servant other than her childhood nanny had ever held her hand in her entire life. There was a time for propriety to be suspended, she realized, and rose to quickly embrace the solicitor.

"Thank you for telling me," she said to the stunned man as she released him and made her way to the bedchamber. "Have a care when you are out, Mr. Fuddleston. I would hate for someone to use you as a means of leverage against the earl."

He nodded and gave her a quick bow. "Thank you, my lady."

CHAPTER 23

*In our times of deepest worry for a friend, it is then that
we realize how very much we esteem one another.*

Mistress Manners' Tips for Every-day Etiquette

Taking a deep breath, she placed her hand on the bedchamber door and pushed it quietly open. Dr. Featherstone was tying off the last of the stitches on Jack's eyebrow, and as she made her way toward the bed, she tried to ignore the fact that it looked as though an animal had been slaughtered on it.

She stood next to Blake, who was still at the doctor's side, likely monitoring every move the man made. He glanced at Ivy and tipped his head in Jack's direction. "The bleeding has stopped; he is stitched. Our only task now is to wait."

Doctor Featherstone moved to the side table and washed his arms and hands in a fresh basin of water. "His Lordship is hardy," he commented over his shoulder as he retrieved a small towel and briskly dried himself. "He will need someone to sleep in here throughout the night, however. Does the man have a proper valet?"

Ivy sighed briefly and closed her eyes. "His valet is young. However, I will admit that the boy seems to know his Lordship very well, and he is incredibly loyal. I will instruct him to sleep in here again, and Mr. Fuddleston in the dressing room. Pug can alert Fuddleston if anything seems amiss."

Doctor Featherstone did not seem impressed, but he finally nodded. "And have someone send for me immediately if he begins to bleed again or seems to worsen."

Ivy couldn't imagine how Jack's condition could possibly worsen; the man hadn't moved a muscle since he was laid out on the bed. She thanked the doctor anyway, and he left.

Ivy looked at Sophia, whose face was pale but firmly set. She clasped one of Jack's hands in her own and brushed a small clump of hair gently off his forehead.

"Sophia," Ivy said softly, "how do you feel about visiting the country estate for some time? Get Jack out of the city for a bit and allow him to heal near the coast."

Sophia looked up at her in some surprise, and her expression gradually shifted, her shoulders relaxing. "I think that sounds wonderful," she murmured, her eyes glossy with unshed tears.

"Your mother would likely enjoy it as well."

"She would, most definitely. And you will join us, naturally." Sophia gave Ivy one definitive nod, as though the matter were already decided.

"I should love to," Ivy murmured and took her first good look at Jack. His face was still a smear of a mess, and he looked as though he'd survived a war, but barely. "We must get him cleaned," she said and looked at Blake. "What would you suggest? His valet is twelve."

Blake chuckled then, and tried to speak but kept laughing. Ivy smiled, and, to her relief, so did Sophia.

"The footman can help you, Lord Blake," Sophia said. "Between the two of you, you'll get him cleaned and stripped of the clothing, at least."

Ivy flushed. "When you get him washed and dressed, I'll help you change the bedding. I believe if we ask anything else of Mrs. Harster tonight, she will expire."

"Do you suppose she would at least be amenable to providing a new stock of towels and some warm water?" Blake asked Ivy, one brow cocked.

"I will see that she brings the towels, and I'll set one of the maids to heating water right away."

Sophia followed Ivy into the dressing room and sank down on a sofa, dropping her head into her hands. Ivy placed a hand on her shoulder for a moment before leaving the room and heading back down the stairs, feeling as though she were moving automatically, without any emotion left. Jack was alive, that counted for something, and she went about the business of sending a footman to the earl's bedchamber and orchestrating details with gratitude that there were details needing orchestrating. It was so much better than sitting and stewing, and she figured that if she sat for more than a moment or two she would dissolve into a puddle of tears.

Because against her better judgment, her feelings for Jack Elliot were growing into something beyond the bounds of acquaintanceship or even friendship. The thought of living in the world without him was dismal, and when she'd seen him that first time lying upon the bed looking broken beyond repair, her heart had broken right along with him.

Steeling her spine, she saw to the business at hand and then retired to the parlor, where she drew some sheets of paper from a small
table and sat, determined to work on a draft for her Mistress Manners
column. Usable content was elusive, of course, and she found herself
drawing drooping flowers and designs and nonsensical things instead.
Her focus was absolutely gone and she wondered if she might be going mad.

Finally, Millie appeared at the parlor door. "Lady Ivy? Miss Elliot
sends for you."

Ivy nodded and replaced the ink bottle and quill. As she passed
the young girl, she stopped. "Millie, are you unwell?"

Millie frowned. "I am fine, Miss. I worry about Pug, though. I
can't find him."

"Have you looked in the mews?"

"Not yet. I was thinking of checking there next."

Ivy drew her brows together. The last thing they needed now was
for Pug to get lost or worse in London. "He is very distraught. Please
do let me know when you find him." Jack was like a father to the boy,
and Pug must have been terrified. She'd been so consumed with her
own emotions that she'd completely forgotten about him.

She reached Jack's bedchamber again, deep in thought. Sophia
had reentered, and Mrs. Harster was inside, gathering bloodied towels and Jack's ruined clothing. "Our head housemaid's mother is a
midwife, my lord," she said to Blake. "The girl, Josephine, can lend a
hand quite efficiently with changing the bedding if you'd like."

Blake nodded. "All right, send her up, but nobody else. The five
of us ought to be able to handle the task." The harried footman stood
to one side, looking a bit worse for the wear but still on his feet.

"Very good, sir. And do send word to me if you would like help from any more of the male employees who might be a bit stronger," she finished, glancing at Ivy and then Sophia.

Blake leveled her with a flat look. "You'll understand completely, madam, when I say that you are all fortunate Miss Elliot hasn't fired the lot of you and begun with fresh staff. Someone in this house is trying to kill your employer and very nearly succeeded this time. I do not want anyone in this room without one of the three of us, Pug, or Fuddleston also present."

Mrs. Harster blanched and nodded with a quick bow. "The warm water will be delivered momentarily, and I placed the clean linens on the bench." She gestured to the foot of the bed and then took her leave.

"Rather autocratic of you," Sophia muttered. "The woman is clearly frazzled and on her last nerve."

"That woman is incompetent in the extreme and doesn't seem to have the wherewithal to manage a household of this size."

"I've seen my share of staff in my life, and at least this woman is kind. She may not be entirely up to her tasks, but the nice ones ought to be treated with respect, at least." Sophia's voice quavered at the last, but her face remained as strong and beautiful as ever. It was ironic, Ivy supposed, that Sophia would probably have been the most effective housekeeper London had ever seen. Those skills would be put to good use when they established their school, which would, regrettably, have to be put aside for the time being.

Blake opened his mouth to retort, but something about Sophia must have given him pause, because he closed his mouth instead and gave her a nod. "My apologies, Miss Elliot, to have offended you."

It was Sophia's turn to appear slightly stunned, and Ivy was grateful to see the arrival of a tall, thin housemaid who bobbed a quick curtsey and introduced herself as Josephine.

The girl, to her credit, marched in at Blake's gesture and began giving instructions as to how they could best maneuver his Lordship to minimize any possible injury and still effectively put clean bedding underneath him. With her expertise, they accomplished the task more quickly than Ivy would have believed possible, and she was professional in her demeanor, so much so that Ivy didn't even have time to be embarrassed that Jack was wearing a nightshirt.

"Thank you, Josephine," Sophia said and nodded to the girl.

"My pleasure, Miss," came the quick reply, accompanied by a flash of pleasure across her features. She gathered the soiled linens and turned to go, but hesitated.

"Is there something else?" Sophia asked her as she wiped her hands on a wet towel.

"Only that my mum is quite good with the ill," Josephine added, "and would help if I sent word. She could be here in a matter of minutes, if ye need, if Doctor Featherstone isn't available, o' course."

"She doesn't carry leeches around, does she?" Blake said, rubbing the back of his neck and then rotating his head from side to side.

Josephine's lips twitched. "No, m'lord. She don't subscribe to that."

"Wise woman," he muttered and began unrolling his sleeves, which were soaked, bloodied, and utterly beyond repair.

Josephine left, and Ivy turned to Blake. "Did he try to use the leeches?" she asked him, horrified.

"He did. I threatened to throw him out the window, and he changed his mind."

"I imagine he did." Ivy felt a genuine smile cross her face for the first time in hours. "You go now and rest some. The supper hour is long gone, and I haven't had nearly the strain you two have experienced. You also, Sophia, go home and get cleaned up."

She shook her head. "I do not want to leave him."

"He is well for now," Ivy told her gently. "Put on fresh clothing, have a cup of tea, and then return. Or have some here. We will rewrite the rule books by having tea around the sickbed."

Sophia snorted a bit, which had been Ivy's aim. She then regarded Blake and dipped into a light curtsey. "I thank you, my lord, for caring for my brother. He means the world to me."

"I would never have supposed it," Blake answered with a half grin. He bowed lightly to her and added, "The pleasure is mine, my lady. He has become a good friend. In fact," he said as he shrugged into his crumpled coat, "he is the only member of the *ton* I like. What does it say for our lot that he is a good person by virtue of the fact that he has never lived among us?"

Ivy dipped her head at him as he took his leave. "Thank you, Lord Blake."

He nodded from the doorway. "Send for me immediately if something happens; otherwise I will check on him in the morning. Has Fuddleston returned yet?"

"I don't believe so," Ivy said.

"Perhaps I can compare notes with him in the morning, and we can get closer to the heart of this." And with that, he strode away.

Sophia was watching the empty doorway, her face pensive.

"What is it?" Ivy asked.

"He is most singular, is he not?"

"That he is. I admit to knowing only superficial things about him; we have shared a dance, that is all. There is depth to his character that catches me by surprise."

Sophia nodded and looked as though she might say more, but instead gave Ivy a quick embrace and turned for the door. "I shall return in thirty minutes. Shall I instruct Mrs. Harster to have a light dinner ready for us? I find now that I'm quite famished."

Ivy didn't think she would ever eat another bite of food in her life, but she nodded anyway. "That sounds delightful."

Finding herself alone with Jack, she located the step stool and climbed up onto the bed. The tears gathered in earnest then. They spilled down her face and onto the clean coverlet that had been pulled up to his shoulders. She laid a hand softly atop his head and allowed herself the luxury of carefully running a curl between her thumb and forefinger. It was likely the only thing soft about the man. Well, that and his affection for Pug and Fuddleston and his family, she supposed. She hoped Millie had been able to locate the boy; that was a new worry to nag at the back of her thoughts.

"Jack Elliot," she murmured, "you must awaken soon, because there are many here who need you. Pug would be bereft if you were to leave, and your mother and Sophia." Would she never stop crying? She had shed more tears in one day than in her entire lifetime. "And me. I need you to stay here, Jack, because we are not finished with our lessons, and it is most unseemly for you to abandon the task prematurely."

His handsome face was battered and swollen, the stitches and bandages garish and frightening. She looked at his chest, though, at its steady rise and fall, and placed her hand over his heart. It beat firmly, as if to reassure her that the body that housed it was merely at rest for a time. Slowly, carefully, she leaned over and placed the gentlest of kisses on his forehead.

"Please wake up," she whispered. "Please. I will never chastise you again for slurping your soup."

CHAPTER 24

In times of emergency or illness, it may become necessary to
swallow one's misgivings in order to aid the afflicted.
Mistress Manners' Tips for Every-day Etiquette

Hazy impressions floated around the edges of Jack's consciousness; snippets flitted in and out of his mind, images of himself
lying prostrate in a carriage, attended by his mother or Sophia, and
sometimes Ivy. He remembered bits of conversation: " . . . *his breathing is still regular . . . he feels warm, do you suppose he is running a
temperature . . . we must get more broth into his system . . . at least he
takes the water well . . .*"

And then there was the blessed tranquillity: a comfortable bed,
wonderfully fresh sea air from an open window. He registered people
helping him drink water, warm broth, and occasionally a tiny bit of
brandy. Just when he was certain he had the strength to open his eyes
fully and converse, he lost all sense of logical thought and floated back
into the realm of impressions and sensations.

Jack awoke one morning to the sound of a bird just outside the window, and he cracked open his eyes, cautiously wondering if he was thinking clearly or still stuck in the baffling fog. The curtains were mostly drawn, but a beam of light filtered through and lit the room enough to afford him a good look at it.

Defining it as "large" would have been an understatement. As far as he could tell, the room was decorated in shades of blue and conspicuously missing a large rectangular object that must once have hung above the fireplace on the opposite wall. The blue-papered walls around the rectangle were lighter than the shape itself, and he wondered what had been removed.

The fireplace boasted a cozy fire that flickered and cast dancing shadows across the floor and walls, and as he slowly propped himself up on one elbow, he noted the opulence of the rest of the room's décor. It had probably once been his grandfather's room, but where?

He eased himself into a sitting position, wincing at the pain that shot through his head. Every muscle in his body felt bruised and battered, and he wondered what on earth had happened. And why was he not at the town house? He searched his mind for the most coherent memory, and the best he could do was the morning after the soiree he had attended with Ivy and his family.

In a flash, he saw himself riding the stallion as though the hounds of hell were at his heels, the rain, the horse rearing . . . and then nothing. How long had he been asleep? Two days? Three?

He was considering the best way to maneuver his screaming muscles from the bed when the door opened softly and Ivy entered. She wore a light dress with an apron, and her hair was pulled into a simple arrangement at her crown; he thought he'd never seen a more beautiful sight in his life.

Her eyes widened as she looked at him, and she dropped a stack of towels she was carrying. She rushed to his side, her face a myriad of emotions, and scrambled up onto the footstool at the side of the bed.

"Jack?" she whispered, and she lifted shaking hands to hold his face gently between her palms. "I can hardly believe it . . . do you recognize me, do you remember anything at all?"

He watched in amazement as her eyes filled with tears that spilled down her cheeks and she blinked, dislodging more. She laughed then, softly, and dropped her hands to his shoulders before gently gathering him in her arms and pulling him into a soft embrace. Stunned, he raised his arms to encircle her, wincing at the movement.

He placed his hands on her back and she trembled slightly, tightening her grip on him and sniffling a bit. "I would imagine this is highly improper," he said, hearing the gravel in his voice and realizing that even his throat felt sore.

She pulled back and again put her hands on his face and shoulders, laughing through her tears. "Oh, it is, but as I've been one of your nursemaids for the last two weeks, I believe I am allowed a small degree of familiarity."

He blinked. *Two weeks?* "Where are we?"

"At your country estate on the coast. We thought it best that we get you out of London for a while, and we decided the sea air might be just the thing to speed your recovery." She drew her brows together and bit her lip, her eyes clouding again. "I was beginning to wonder if you ever would. Recover, that is."

"Two weeks?"

She nodded. "Your mother and Sophia are here, of course. And we also brought with us a very competent maid, Josephine, as well as a new young doctor from London who is privy to all of medicine's newest discoveries. Anthony Blake has visited several times and arranged for a retinue of guards to patrol the estate day and night."

He blinked again. "Two weeks?" he repeated.

"Fuddleston is in London for the moment, ensuring the continued operation of your affairs and looking for new leads, and will return tomorrow. And Pug sleeps in the adjoining room. He was most distraught after the accident. He hid in the stable loft for a good sixteen hours before Millie finally found him buried in a pile of scratchy hay."

She smiled. "I must go find the others; they will be so relieved." She paused. "*I* am so relieved. We aren't anywhere near finished with our lessons yet."

He chuckled then, and his head pounded. Wincing, he put his hand to the side of his head and ran it around the back, feeling a ridge of what he assumed were stitches.

"Two large gashes," she said when he moved his hand to his face and felt the bump of stitches along his eyebrow. "One at the back of your head, and this one, which crosses down over your eye and onto your nose." She ran a fingertip along the bridge of his nose, and as his brain continued to clear, he decided a few scars and gashes might not be such a bad thing.

She winced. "There was so much blood. And you were bruised from head to toe. No broken bones that the doctor could ascertain, but as battered as you were, it was probably almost a kindness that you slept through the bulk of the aftermath. Do you remember at all what happened?"

"I was thrown from my horse while riding in the park." The image returned, more forcefully this time, and he remembered a moment of panic as he fell to the ground.

"Yes." She took his hand in both of hers and clasped it. "It wasn't an accident, Jack. Someone had placed a nail under the saddle."

His heart thumped, but didn't find himself at all surprised. "Percival."

"We suspect as much, but Mr. Fuddleston is still searching for information that will link him to the crimes. We do know that the cook's assistant was the one who slipped the poison into your drink, but he has disappeared, and we are unable to trace him to gain more information, even if he had more to give us."

He waited for a surge of anger, but perhaps his body was simply too weary to allow for it. "Given that Blake has positioned an army outside, one might assume we'll be safe here for a while." He smiled, or tried to, anyway. It felt odd and pulled at all of the scratches and stitches on his face.

"Jack, before I summon the others, I owe you an apology. I'm afraid this may be all my fault."

He lifted a brow in question, marveling at the fact that simple expressions required so many facial muscles to produce.

"The day you found my notes in the library, Millie had just told me about overhearing a conversation between Cook's assistant and someone in the dark she couldn't see. I was so angry with you over discovering my secret that it slipped my mind. I ought to have followed you out of the house to tell you. And then we attended the soiree that night and I was so irritated that you spoke well and had deceived me about your abilities, and I should have—"

He placed his forefinger across her lips and smiled. "That would be the day I kissed you in the library."

She flushed and nodded.

"Well then, I shouldn't be surprised at all that important information slipped your mind. It happens all the time."

Her lips quirked into a half smile, and she closed her eyes briefly with a little shake of the head. "All the time, does it? You kiss ladies senseless on a regular basis, then?"

"Senseless. I like that. And yes, on a regular basis. Daily. Hourly, even."

"Most inappropriate, my lord. I do not believe I approve."

"And I think I like that you do not approve."

Her gaze locked with his, and for a moment he had an insane urge to kiss her senseless again. She finally blinked and broke the spell.

"I must find the others," she whispered, placing her palm one last time at his cheek. "It wouldn't be well done of me at all to keep you to myself."

"I find that I don't mind in the least."

She smiled and again encircled his neck for an embrace that he wished would last forever. He pulled her close, splaying his fingers across her back and tightening his grip when she moved to pull back.

"One more moment, just one," he whispered in her ear and was gratified to hear her sigh.

"I . . . we . . ."

"Shhh." He closed his eyes and inhaled deeply, ignoring the pain in his ribs in favor of appreciating the subtle smell of the lilac soap he had come to associate with her. He felt a little foolish to be sitting in bed, wounded and as helpless as a child, but the reward of such exquisite pleasure as holding Ivy Carlisle in his arms for a few moments outweighed any masculine embarrassment.

"I am so very glad you are well, my lord," she whispered, and his heart tripped.

"As am I, my lady." He turned his lips toward her neck and inhaled her scent one last time before she pulled away.

She held him firmly at arm's length. "Most improper of me to have been so forward," she murmured.

"You could close the door, and everyone will assume I am still unconscious," he said with a wink, and she blushed to the roots of her hair. He fought a chuckle when she jumped down from the stool and made her way to the door, picking up the towels she'd dropped upon entry.

"Absolutely incorrigible," she said over her shoulder to him. "I can see we still have loads of work ahead of us." She smiled as she looked back at him before leaving, shaking her head. "Most improper of me," he heard her mutter as she left the room.

CHAPTER 25

*Convalescence for the wounded or ill should be a gentle
period of calm reflection and mild behavior, on the
part of both the affected and his associates.*

Mistress Manners' Tips for Every-day Etiquette

J ack moved around slowly, following his mother's sage advice to re-
cuperate at a sedate pace. The first two days were difficult; he found
himself exhausted with the effort it took to climb stairs and would
have been frustrated in the extreme were it not for the constant relief
and joy on his loved ones' faces.

He familiarized himself with the country estate, which was large
and beautiful. A skeleton staff resided year-round, and historically,
when the family had been in residence, other help was hired as
needed from the village. The doctor Ivy had brought with them from
London, Doctor Miller, was an amiable sort, reminding Jack of an
eager puppy. He was slight of build and cheery of disposition, but
his demeanor changed and he was a consummate professional when
conducting his duties as the earl's physician. Jack found grudging

admiration for the intelligent young man, despite the fact that he seemed annoyingly happy day in, day out.

When he had awakened, his mother and Sophia had been overjoyed, of course, and tearful. Mary explained that upon their arrival, she had removed the large portrait of Jack's grandfather that hung over the mantelpiece in his bedchambers. In her first official act as the mother of the earl, she had ordered it and all other likenesses of the man relegated to the attic, and Sophia, to her delight, had found a few portraits of their father that had been painted when he was a child. Those now hung in positions of prominence in the home, and Sophia and Ivy were altering and tweaking things subtly, creating a haven that reflected the new earl and his family rather than the old one. The staff seemed to be breathing a collective sigh of relief—they were enamored of Jack's mother, and for that, he was thrilled.

He was as happy as he'd been before the radical turn his life had taken, and he felt strangely at peace. They were situated on the coast, perhaps that was the difference, and the fresh, clear sea air was familiar and welcoming. He thought even his mother looked a bit healthier—she was still thin, but her cheeks had filled out some and had taken on a healthy glow that he couldn't remember ever seeing on her before. He determined to be sure she remained at the estate as long as possible, spending only a limited amount of time in London. The city air was undoubtedly bad for her, and here in the country, she didn't have to worry about impressing the right person or insulting the wrong one. She had taken up residence during the days in one of the upper rooms, setting up paints and easels, finally able to pursue her talents without worrying about how she was going to put food on the table for herself and her daughter.

Clarence Fuddleston kept him updated on affairs from London, and Jack was gladder than ever that he had offered the little man the position. He trusted him implicitly, and Fuddleston seemed to recognize it. There was an air of quiet confidence about his man of affairs that put Jack's mind at ease. The weight of responsibility for the earldom was settling on Jack's shoulders, but it was oddly comfortable, and he finally acknowledged the fact that it wasn't going to go away. If he hadn't had Fuddleston at his side, though, he readily admitted he would have been completely lost.

He was taking a walk on the grounds outside the home a week after his "awakening," as the others were calling it, deep in thought about Ivy. She had retreated to a comfortable, appropriate distance and seemed to be taking great pains to avoid being alone with him. He smiled in spite of himself as he looked out over the land that was his as far as the eye could see. She was reverting to that which was safe for her, and she'd even begun hinting at the fact that when they returned and he launched himself into Society in earnest she was planning to redouble her efforts at finding him a wonderful bride.

He wasn't offended that she had taken herself out of the running. In truth, she had never included herself there at all. He was amused. Lady Ivy Carlisle's well-ordered life did not involve the prospect of marriage to a sea-dog-turned-nobleman. His only fear was that she herself would jump at marriage to someone else—her blond paragon, Lord Hovley, for instance—rather than admit her feelings for him. The attraction was undeniable, and until most recently, their time together had become a thing of laughter and genuine joy.

And what of his future plans? He had become less consumed with finding a loophole in the contract his grandfather had concocted, had actually been happy to conveniently shift those former thoughts to the side for the time being. He still felt at a loss, however, as he attempted to fit his large, active personality into its new role of relative leisure and meaningless pursuit. It didn't sit well with him, and he feared he would go mad if he had nothing constructive or meaningful to occupy his time.

Sophia and Ivy still had hopes for their girls' school, and they planned daily together, sketching pictures and sharing ideas. He would be a part of it, but it wasn't his project.

He drew his brows together as he paused and continued to search the horizon, looking for something elusive he couldn't name. The stitches in his eyebrow pulled and his head still maintained a dull ache, but he felt his strength returning slowly. He honestly admitted to himself that the thought of someone sincerely wanting him dead weighed on him more than he would have imagined.

"Strolling again?" Ivy said as she approached him from the house, wrapped in a lacy green shawl that matched her eyes. That he even made note of such a detail would have had him snorting in disgust weeks earlier.

"I find myself restless if I'm indoors for long periods of time," he told her and shifted slightly so that his back was to the sun and shielded her eyes by placing her in his large shadow.

She smiled. "A true sailor. You would certainly be missed here if you returned to the sea."

"Would you miss me?"

"Of course! I have come to appreciate our association very much."

"You deliberately mistake my meaning, Ivy."

"Not at all." She sobered a bit and met his gaze with a frank one of her own. "You intend to leave, Jack. And it is a matter of self-preservation that I rein in any special regard I may have for you."

"The idea of leaving is losing much of its appeal," he admitted to her quietly.

Her eyes widened, and she looked away from him, thoughtfully chewing on her lip. "Have a care with my heart, Jack Elliot," she finally murmured, still looking away. "I was fully content to form an alliance like my parents'. If I become accustomed to . . . to . . . the thought that there might be something more, and then have it snatched away, I believe I will become a most unhappy woman."

He shifted again, moving fractionally closer to shield her from a gust of wind that came in over the water.

"I've taught you everything you need to know." She finally met his eyes. "And truthfully, I doubt you ever really needed me."

His heart picked up its pace, and he felt something akin to panic that she might be attempting to end their arrangement. "I've always needed you, Ivy; you cannot just leave. And what of my mother and Sophia?"

She knit her brows and winced. "I can continue to help them if they require it, and Sophia and I are the best of friends by now, of course, so I will see them regularly."

"But not me."

She shrugged, and he thought for a moment she might cry.

"What are you running from?" he murmured and put a finger beneath her chin.

He tipped her head back, and she met his eyes, and there was no mistaking the sheen of moisture in hers. "You. My feelings are engaged to a dangerous degree, Jack. You will eventually tire of your ridiculous life in London and find a way to set sail, leaving this far behind for months at a time. And it would leave me with a broken heart, because I very much like being with you."

He thumbed a tear that rolled down her cheek. "Why don't you let me decide what I do and do not want?"

She shook her head, and her breath hitched. "I cannot afford to." She took a step back from him and he followed, clasping her arm.

"You are not finished yet," he said. "You will make a liar of your grandmother, who gave my grandfather her word on his deathbed that you would see this thing through."

"Very well." She lifted her chin. "But we will return to decorum and propriety. I will fulfil my obligation and find you a suitable young lady who won't mind so much staying behind while her husband leaves. There are a dozen who would love to snag an earl and couldn't care one whit over whether or not it is a love match."

He narrowed his eyes, his frustration rising. "At what point did you decide you were entitled to make decisions for me?"

"It is for the best, Jack. You must admit it!"

He gritted his teeth. There had been no mistaking her feelings for him when she had entered that bedroom and seen him sitting up, awake. He had realized then, on some level, that he wanted Ivy Carlisle by his side forever. To be his wife—his friend, his lover, the mother of his children.

"Very well." He still held fast to her arm. "We will return to London and have our wonderful parties, and you will look for other women you think I might find the least objectionable. And while we are doing all of this, you will be thinking of one thing."

"And that would be?"

"This."

He pulled her into his arms and plunged his hand into her hair, lowering his mouth to hers and savoring the experience. He kissed her well and thoroughly and nearly groaned aloud when she responded.

She might say all the right words she felt she needed to, but she couldn't deny her heart. Had she objected to his kiss, he would have pulled back and given her the freedom she said she needed in order to guard herself from pain. Ridiculous, really, because he had no intention of ever causing her any. But she met him halfway and placed a hand at the back of his neck, as much a participant as a receiver.

"So," he said unsteadily against her mouth as he finally broke the contact, "while you are scouting the room for my future wife, you will think on the fact that you are handing her this instead of keeping it for yourself."

"Jack," she whispered brokenly, "you are unfair."

"No, my lady, you are the one who denies not only yourself, but me as well." He released her and looked at her kiss-swollen mouth and tear-filled eyes, fighting every urge to pull her back into his arms. Instead, he performed a feat of herculean effort and turned, leaving her in the gentle breeze.

He made his way angrily into the house and searched for Fuddleston, who was in the library. "You mentioned visiting the tenants?" he said.

Fuddleston looked up from his ledger and blinked at him before nodding. "Yes," he answered. "I believe it would be a wise thing to do before returning to the city."

"We shall go now, then. How soon can you be ready?"

Fuddleston opened his mouth and closed it again, glancing down at the books. "Now, I suppose, sir."

"Stop calling me 'sir.' I told you to call me 'Jack.' Now fetch your coat and whatever else we will need."

Fuddleston rose from the desk with a nod, although he eyed Jack with some suspicion. "Is everything well, my lo—Jack?" He flushed.

Jack raised a shoulder, tempted for a moment to confide in him. He finally shook his head. Fuddleston would have no better insight into a woman's mind than he did. "I am fine," he finally said. "Let us do this before we lose daylight. I should like to see the condition of the tenants' housing. If my grandfather's legacy with my family is any indication of how he cared for those on his land, I am guessing there is much work to be done."

Besides, he was going to have to keep himself busy while he plotted his future. And contemplate the most effective ways to convince a woman to follow her instincts rather than habit. Because if there was only one certainty in life, he had realized it was this: Ivy Carlisle was his, and he didn't want any other. And he would crawl through Dante's proverbial pit before seeing her with another man.

Lady Ivy had set out to create a gentleman, and she was going to find she had succeeded. After a fashion, at least. His frustration gave way to determination as he began to formulate a plan. By the time he left the house with Fuddleston, he was whistling. "Clarence, my good man," he said as he clapped the baffled solicitor on the shoulder, "let us do some good today."

CHAPTER 26

Fear is frequently the most powerful of
motivators; to defeat it is wise.

Mistress Manners' Tips for Every-day Etiquette

One week passed in a flurry of comfortable activity, and Ivy smiled as she passed the library on her way to the parlor where she was to meet Sophia. Jack and Fuddleston were elbow-deep in documents and drawings of the tenant housing, planning improvements to many of the old structures and replacements for others that were uninhabitable. Jack had returned from his initial inspection of the properties on his land the week before, his face an absolute thundercloud. Fuddleston had looked equally grim, and ever since, they had been men obsessed with a worthy cause.

It came as no surprise to anyone that the old earl had neglected his tenants to an extreme. Jack had reported to Ivy, Sophia, and Mary that there were entire families living in absolute squalor. Jack had a new air about him, a true sense of purpose. She was able to picture him at sea, running an entire ship and its rowdy crew. She had hopes that this venture might provide him with that sense of meaningful pursuit he seemed to have been struggling to find in London. But she couldn't shake the feelings she'd had when they had toured the maritime museum, the impressions that his first love would always be the sea, and that it was where he truly belonged.

Ivy entered the parlor to find Sophia reading a letter, pacing before the hearth. She glanced up at Ivy and said, "We must return to London if we wish to secure the property for the school. The owner is threatening to sell it to someone else if we do not claim it immediately."

Ivy nodded and tapped her finger against her lip. "I believe Jack and Fuddleston are finishing their business for now. They need to go back to London to secure materials for the tenant repairs. It's as good a time as any, I suppose. I hate to take your mother back so soon, though."

Sophia nodded. "I agree. Perhaps she'd like to remain here."

"When we return, I will accept invitations to the last few balls of the Season, and we can then consider you and Jack well and truly launched." She smiled at Sophia, who rolled her eyes and then looked at Ivy for a moment in clear speculation.

"What are you going to do about Jack?"

"I'm sure I don't know what you mean."

"Ivy, you cannot fool me, so do not try."

"He kissed me again," she admitted.

Sophia's eyes lit up. "I should hope he did! He watches you every moment of the day, you know. And when you leave a room, it is as though his mind has gone with you."

Ivy's heart thumped in response, and to her dismay, she felt herself sinking into the abyss. She absolutely would not fall in love with Jack Elliot.

Sophia folded the letter she'd been reading and brushed her skirts. "You can deny yourself happiness, but I'm sure I don't understand why you would." She made her way to the door.

"I am finding my feelings most conflicted," Ivy said softly.

Sophia paused at the doorway and turned back to Ivy. "In what way?"

"I am afraid."

"There is an element of fear in every worthwhile endeavor, is there not? We can never escape it entirely."

She left, and Ivy stood alone in the parlor, feeling bereft and miserable and desperately wanting comfort from the one man she was trying to avoid. She touched her fingertips to her lips and remembered the kiss and the breathlessness that had ensued. She had nearly sunk to the ground when he'd left her outside, her knees weak and her heart pounding.

She was playing a dangerous game with a man who was probably sincere in his affection for her but who might well tire of his responsibilities on land and leave for good. There were no guarantees, and Ivy had lived her life on guarantees. If she did everything that was expected of her, if she bridled her passions, reined in her sense of humor and her impulsive side, she would make a suitable match to a suitable gentleman and then they would together have suitable children.

Jack Elliot had turned her well-ordered existence on its head.

He was suitable in that he was an earl, of course, but he made her laugh quite loudly, he teased and cajoled, he regaled her with stories of adventures on the high seas that he really shouldn't share with a lady, and he kissed her until she thought she would die from the pleasure of it. He drew out of her the impulsive aspect she'd worked so hard to control, making her believe it was perfectly acceptable to put one's schedule aside and enjoy a picnic instead.

And he supported her writing. True to his word, he had not told a soul that she was the voice behind Mistress Manners, but he occasionally asked if he might read her drafts, and he made comments that drew laughter from her along with flushes of pride. She found herself wanting to make him smile and was ridiculously gratified when she achieved it.

"Ivy?"

She turned at his voice in the doorway, and her breath caught at his appearance. He was dressed as a lord of the manor, the bruises on his face fading. The scar across his eyebrow and onto his nose only made him all the more handsome, which made absolutely no sense to her whatsoever. She had thought to pity him, had wondered if she would need to reassure him that he would still be attractive to eligible females, and instead she found herself marveling at the fact that he was more dashing than ever.

"Yes?"

"Sophia has told me we must return to London?"

Ivy nodded with a sigh. "This has been a rather lovely holiday from the city, has it not? I hate to return."

He eyed her for a moment, and she could have sworn there was a twinkle in his eye. "Well, we have much to accomplish upon our return. Sophia and I are most anxious to be presented officially to the *ton*."

Ivy gave him a flat look. "Indeed."

"If you believe you can manage it, we will pack up and leave by morning's first light." He gave her a bright smile and tipped his head in a bow to her before leaving the room.

What on earth was he about? She didn't trust the look in his eye for a moment, but she shook her head and left the parlor, making her way upstairs to her bedchamber to begin preparing for the return trip to London. She was agitated and couldn't define exactly why, only that she knew something odd was on the horizon.

Ivy's mother smiled when she returned home, and Ivy wondered if perhaps some of the sting of Caroline's behavior was finally receding. Her mother asked questions about the earl's estate and holdings, of course, but also asked after Mary's welfare. She then told Ivy to be sure to attend the Norringtons' ball on Thursday evening because it was certain to be an absolute crush.

It was just as well that Ivy had already been planning the Norringtons' event as the perfect place for Jack and Sophia to make an official appearance. They had yet to attend a large function, and this would be the first that also involved dancing. They had only had a few rounds of lessons; she hoped desperately that it had been enough.

Ivy left instructions for her maid to unpack her trunk and then went to Sophia's house. Mary had stayed behind at the country estate, and Ivy genuinely felt it was just as well. Mary's acceptance by the *ton* was not as crucial as Sophia's if the older woman's intention was to live the bulk of her life outside of London.

Sophia was just exiting the front door when Ivy arrived, and Sophia climbed into the carriage next to her with a light in her eye and a becoming blush to her cheeks. "We are about to do something amazing, Ivy!"

Ivy smiled, feeling the excitement settling into her bones. "This is the first monumental thing I've done, Sophia. Nana is so proud!"

The ride to the building they had selected was quick and un-eventful, and when they arrived, Ivy's optimism faltered just a bit. "There is much to be done, isn't there?" she murmured.

"Take heart." Sophia linked her arm within Ivy's. "We can do difficult things."

Ivy smiled at her friend, noting not for the first time her incredible beauty and realizing that Sophia's inner glow was all the more stunning. She had arisen from the ashes of gut-wrenching poverty and was turning her experiences into something worthwhile. "I am most fortunate to know you, Sophia Elliot," Ivy said with a burning sensation in her eyes. "And I am so grateful to call you my friend. I've never really had one, you know."

Sophia's eyes widened, and she shook Ivy's arm with her own. "No tears, Ivy! You mustn't start this, or we will simply sit down here on the roadside and cry!"

Ivy laughed as Sophia bustled them ahead to the doorway, but not before she saw a sheen in Sophia's eyes that matched her own. As they toured the rundown building and began making notes for improvements and redesign, the only negative lurking at the back of her mind was a worry that by bringing Jack back to London, they had also brought him back to the lions' den. She only hoped that the guards Anthony Blake had secured could keep him safe. The alternative didn't bear contemplation; the thought of repeating the agony that had accompanied Jack's last accident was more than her heart could manage.

Chapter 27

*Accidents can be horribly frightening, but one should
endeavour to handle them with grace and dignity.*

Mistress Manners' Tips for Every-day Etiquette

Jack entered his town house library and extended his hand to Lord
Anthony Blake. Fuddleston had informed him that Blake had taken
the attacks on Jack's life most seriously, and together the two men
were hunting down every possible lead they could find.

"Glad to see you looking so well, Jack," Blake said.

"I appreciate your efforts on my behalf," Jack said, motioning toward the seats flanking the hearth. "Have you learned anything new?"

"A few things of note." Blake settled into the chair. "I hate to be
the bearer of bad news, but I believe your father's cousin may indeed
be behind the attempts on your life."

Jack's heart sank a bit, and it surprised him that he felt a sting of
betrayal. "I suspected as much. What makes you believe it to be true?"

"I ran down the contact who communicated with your cook's
assistant through a few eyewitnesses who saw him on the night in

question. He eventually gave up the name of another 'businessman' who frequents haunts on the docks and takes bribes from noblemen to conduct their dirty business. He confirmed that a missive originating from Percival Elliot's home was behind both the poisoning and the nail under the saddle."

"And would we be able to secure an arrest with this information?"

Blake thought for a moment. "We do not have the original note," he admitted, "and without the written evidence, all else is just hearsay, the word of a dockside thug against a nobleman. But Fuddleston and I do have one other plan," he continued. "We've offered a bribe of our own to this dockside 'businessman.' If your cousin should make another request, we can nab him or his representative in the act."

Jack nodded. "I do worry about my family. I have a guard accompanying Sophia all hours of the day, but I confess, I would not be surprised if my cousin attempted to use my sister as leverage against me."

Blake nodded solemnly, and Jack saw his jaw tighten at the mention of danger to Sophia. "We will be vigilant, Jack, be assured of it." He rose and turned to take his leave. "Have a care, then, and I will inform you at once should we discover anything pertinent."

Jack slowly walked over to the large hearth and leaned his shoulder against the mantle. So it had been Percival all along. He was not in the least surprised. The fear in his gut for his family, however, was very real and he felt a sense of frustration at his helplessness. It would hardly do to tip his hand and confront Percival directly, although he dearly wanted to. The man would deny everything, of course, and then all hopes of catching him in the act of hiring an assassin would be lost.

He closed his eyes and rubbed his hand across the bridge of his nose, which was still tender. He wanted Ivy. Wanted to talk with her about Blake's comments, would relish the fact that she would simply *be* there with him. He had no idea what her choice of phrase might be, but he knew the tone she would use. It would be calming and full of reassurance. And he would look at her and become delightfully distracted and then kiss her again. . . .

What a complicated tangle his life had become! He was watching for killers over one shoulder while trying to win the affections of a woman who was afraid to trust her own feelings. Throw the welfare of his beautiful, feisty sister into the mix, not to mention his ailing mother, and he had his hands quite full.

Life at sea was ever so much simpler.

Ivy and Sophia had just completed a most successful meeting with the man who would oversee the repairs and redesign of the girls' home building. As they had described their needs, he was at first reluctant to take orders from two women, but then Nana had arrived at the offices and taken the situation in hand. Before Ivy really knew what had happened, the man had gathered all of their notes and diagrams and promised to have a plan drawn by week's end.

Nana winked at the girls when they left the offices, kissed Ivy, and then announced she was fatigued and must return home. The girls stood next to Ivy's carriage for a moment, watching as the dowager climbed into her conveyance and left them as quickly as she had come.

"Well," Sophia said, "I am duly impressed."

"Indeed. And I can guarantee you, she's not fatigued." Ivy said. "I only mentioned to her briefly that we were scheduled to conduct this meeting today and told her we would care for the bulk of the details ourselves. All we require of her and Jack in the next day or so is to sign the official documents and arrange for the funds."

Sophia knit her brows together. "She must have realized we would encounter resistance."

Ivy nodded. "And now she has removed herself again so that we might do this on our own."

"She is a lovely lady," Sophia said.

"That she certainly is." Ivy smiled at the empty street where Nana's carriage had stood. She and Sophia were preparing to climb into their own carriage when a scream echoed down the crowded street.

A wagon pulled by two enormous horses barreled toward them. The driver held tight to the reins, his hat pulled low and the collar of his jacket turned up, hiding any glimpse of his face and neck. He continued on his breakneck course, pulling the horses roughly to the side as they reached the women, causing the wagon to careen crazily into the carriage with an enormous crash.

Ivy shoved Sophia to the side as the entire carriage toppled, yanking the horses askew and spooking them thoroughly as they thrashed at the air and screamed. The falling conveyance knocked Ivy to the ground, and her head spun madly as she stared into the road where the offending horses had entangled themselves in a crowd outside a shop, the wagon hanging off one axle. The driver himself was nothing more than a figure in the distance, fleeing down the street and away from the scene.

"Are you hurt?" Sophia asked Ivy and gasped as she put her gloved hand to Ivy's temple. She withdrew her hand to reveal a smear of blood, and Ivy wondered why she didn't feel any pain. She also wondered why Sophia had doubled, and there were now two of her friend swimming before her eyes.

"Hold this," Sophia ordered and placed Ivy's fingers over a hand-kerchief against the side of her head. "Are you injured anywhere else?"

Ivy frowned as her temple suddenly began to throb.

"You awright, miss?" a young boy asked as he surveyed the damage and another man attempted to right the flailing horses.

"We need to summon a cab," Sophia told the boy and rose unsteadily to her feet. "Did anyone recognize the wagon driver?"

There was now quite a crowd gathered around the overturned carriage, a sea of faces that Ivy didn't recognize. Voices blended together; nobody seemed to know who the other driver was, and should somebody send for a doctor?

Ivy looked up at Sophia, trying to focus on her face as Sophia conferred with the man who had been acting as their guard throughout the day. He tripped all over himself in apologizing to Sophia, who waved a hand at him impatiently. "Fetch us a cab," she told him, "and then give the driver my brother's address." He dashed off to follow her orders.

"Come, Ivy." Sophia stooped to help Ivy stand, tugging at a portion of Ivy's dress that was trapped beneath the carriage. She tore it free with a rip of fabric and then put an arm about Ivy's shoulders, guiding her to the roadside, where a cab pulled up.

If only she weren't so dizzy. Ivy fought a wave of nausea and leaned heavily against Sophia as their frantic guard helped them into the carriage.

"Would you rather go home, Ivy?" Sophia asked her after insuring that the driver had Jack's address.

Ivy squinted and then closed her eyes, leaning against Sophia's shoulder. "Nobody at home; my mother is at tea with Lady Dresden," she mumbled. The cab lurched into traffic and maneuvered past the mess they were leaving behind.

Ivy frowned. "I must have the horses and the carriage returned home. My father will be most upset if the horses are harmed."

"The horses will be fine," Sophia muttered. "When we get to Jack's, I'll have his footman deliver a message to your house. And then perhaps we should send for your Nana?"

"I do not want to worry her." Ivy closed her eyes and wished the pain in her head would subside. "I must have just been knocked by the carriage—I will be fine." The fog was indeed beginning to lift, and her thoughts became a little more focused. "Did you happen to see who the man was?"

"No."

"Well," Ivy said, trying for a levity she definitely did not feel, "either someone still doesn't like your brother, or he's angry at us for opening the school."

The carriage finally increased in speed as they pulled through the bulk of the chaos they were leaving behind.

"You saved my life, Ivy." Sophia's voice trembled.

"Oh, that," Ivy said and was glad when Sophia chuckled. "I perform such amazing feats on a daily basis."

The ride to Jack's town house was quick, and Sophia ushered Ivy up the front stairs. Watkins's face registered surprise that he quickly managed to squelch as Sophia took Ivy into the parlor, snapping instructions for someone to find the earl as she eased her down onto a settee.

Ivy's heartbeat quickened at Jack's entrance, and the look on his face was one of sheer panic. "I am fine," she said as he sank down to his knees and grasped her hand, which still held Sophia's handkerchief to her temple.

"Let me see," he murmured.

"I'm sure it's nothing," Ivy said, shrugging a shoulder. "Truly, it just hurts a bit. I'm no longer seeing two of everything."

Jack closed his eyes briefly at her pronouncement and shook his head. "Sophia, will you have Watkins send for Lord Blake, please? I want him to hear any details you can recall." He gently pulled Ivy's hand away and brushed his finger lightly over her temple. "You'll have a lovely knot here for a while, but at least the bleeding seems to have stopped. Where was that deuced guard?"

"He was right there with us, my lord." Ivy wanted to crawl into Jack's lap and sleep for a bit. "Everything happened so quickly—there was nothing for the guard to do."

"I'm going to kill him." Jack's expression hadn't changed much, but his tone was like ice.

"There was nothing he could have done," Ivy repeated.

Jack shook his head. "Not the guard."

Ivy frowned as Jack rose and gave instructions to Mrs. Harster to fetch a cloth and basin of cold water.

"You cannot kill your cousin, Jack." Ivy had the wherewithal to be worried he might to do something rash.

"Maybe not today," he answered mildly as he stood looking at her, but she wasn't deceived by the neutral expression. His fists were clenched, and she didn't figure that was a good sign.

He was quiet, his expression grim until Mrs. Harster returned with his requested items. He dipped the small cloth into the water and wrung it out, placing it against Ivy's head. "Does it hurt much?" he asked her, his tone quiet and again deceptively calm.

"No, Jack, truly." She grasped the wrist that held the cloth to her temple. "Only just a bit."

"I shall have Cook put on the kettle for tea," Mrs. Harster said, and Jack nodded once in her direction. When she left the room and they were alone, Jack reached up and placed his lips to Ivy's forehead. She closed her eyes, reveling in his nearness and that scent that was so uniquely his.

"This cannot continue." Jack softly touched the knot that was forming on the side of her head.

"Indeed not," Ivy said, trying to lighten the mood, "because what will everyone think when I show up at events looking like a pugilist?"

His lips quirked, and she hoped she had taken his mind off the tantalizing topic of throttling his cousin. "Perhaps I should tie Percival's hands behind his back and let you have the first swing at him," he suggested.

Drat. The mood was clearly not lightened. "We will get to the bottom of all of this, and you and your family will be finally left at peace."

"I am concerned that something catastrophic will occur before we can get to that point." Jack palmed her cheek and frowned. "I could not bear to lose you."

Ivy shook her head. "I don't believe I was the intended target, Jack. It was Sophia. I just happened to be in the way."

He gritted his teeth and looked away.

"Perhaps the goal is to frighten you into giving up the earldom?" she suggested.

"This is a nightmare," he muttered and dropped his hand. "And I believe the doctor should examine you."

"That is entirely unnecessary. I am feeling much refreshed."

Jack stood and left the room; she heard him giving instructions for someone to send for Josephine's mother. Maybe a little pampering would be fine, she thought as she put her hand to the knot on her temple and choked back a gasp. She was lucky she wasn't dead, that much was so very true, but now she nearly burst into tears at the thought of how she must appear. Showing up at *ton* events with a goose egg on the side of one's head was just *not* the thing.

CHAPTER 28

Betrayal at the hands of one's relations can be the
bitterest of pills. There are times when one would
be well advised to consider the source.

Mistress Manners' Tips for Every-day Etiquette

Lord Anthony Blake rang the bell early the next morning. Jack, who was actually up before Watkins, opened the door himself and welcomed the man into the parlor, offering him coffee or tea.

"No, thank you." Blake eyed him for a moment before moving to the seat Jack had indicated. "I apologize for the early hour, but I do come bearing news. We've caught the responsible party."

"Excellent." Jack nodded, feeling a sense of relief. "What did the brigand say when you cornered him? What is the plan for prosecution?"

"Well, the identity of the guilty party has come as a bit of a surprise. Your cousin's wife hired the boy who supplied the poison and also contacted your former groom to orchestrate the sabotaged saddle that led to your accident in the park. She was also behind the attack yesterday on your sister and Lady Ivy. She was having them followed.

It was while delivering those instructions that Mrs. Elliot's servant was captured. It seems that when she realized further attempts would likely be impossible because of the increased security protection surrounding you, she set up the attack on your sister."

"Clista was behind it?" Jack's head was reeling, but he wondered why. It wasn't as though he felt such actions to be beyond his cousin's wife; Ivy had mistrusted her from the beginning.

Blake eyed him with something akin to sympathy.

"I cannot thank you enough for your quick action in this matter," Jack told him. "I was becoming alarmed in the extreme for my family's safety."

"Under the threat of legal proceedings, to say nothing of their ruin in Society, Mr. and Mrs. Percival Elliot have opted to flee to the Continent rather than face a court verdict and possible deportation to Australia. I will keep you abreast of any new developments, of course, but am hopeful you will now see the end of your troubles."

Jack hadn't realized how much worry had been hovering in the back of his mind from the night he'd realized someone had tried to poison him. For a man whose life was well-ordered and predictable, it had been an unsettling heaviness that he had carried without even acknowledging it.

"Again, I thank you," he told Blake and stood, gripping his friend's hand in both of his own.

The day of the Norringtons' ball was fast approaching, and, to Ivy's immense relief, Lord Blake had saved the day and exposed the woman (woman!) behind the attempts on Jack's life. Ivy sniffed a bit and took perverse satisfaction at the thought of Clista Elliot sitting in a dank cell at Newgate. It would never happen, of course; she was long gone from the country and could never return, but the image of her clapped in irons made Ivy smile nonetheless.

Jack had received a letter from his mother. She was happy and doing well, and she had even been invited to tea by a few local gentle-women who were "very amiable" and appreciated Mary's knowledge of finer fabrics and sewing techniques. Ivy had to admit that she was relieved Mary preferred the countryside and they wouldn't have to worry about whether someone was going to cut or embarrass her.

"Now, then," Ivy said as she sat with Jack in the library—with the door wide open to the hallway—"I had intended to review all of the things we've learned over these past several weeks, but you, my lord, seem to have become a master pupil."

Jack grinned at her, and her heart stopped. "Only because I have the world's best tutor."

"You are incorrigible." She smiled in spite of herself.

"And you wouldn't have me any other way."

Ivy supposed that was true enough. She found herself drawn to the elements of his character that had nothing to do with manners or breeding and everything to do with just . . . him. "You have chosen your attire for the ball tomorrow night?"

He nodded. "I will look every inch the dashing earl. And might I assume you are ready to point me in the direction of a few eligible ladies?"

Ivy's heart sank. But what had she expected, really? He wasn't going to follow her around forever, and she had made it very clear that she wasn't interested in marriage to him.

"Yes." she forced a smile. "I'm certain we shall find a few who will not mind the thought of her husband being away at sea for the better part of their life together."

"Excellent." He leaned forward and stacked some papers on his desk. "I suppose we are finished for the day, and unless you send word otherwise, I shall see you tomorrow evening at the Norringtons'."

Ivy opened her mouth to say something and closed it again. She supposed it was wise that he not invite her to stay and have tea or ask her opinion on décor for the town house. Just because that was the pattern they had followed since their first ride together in Hyde Park didn't mean it was something that should continue. He would soon belong to another woman, and although her stomach turned at the thought, she was at a loss about how to fix it.

He glanced up at her from his desk, one brow raised. "Is there something else?"

"No, my lord."

It is too late, she realized with a sinking sensation. She had already lost her heart to the man—it didn't matter whether she married him or not. She had fallen in love with the sailor, and not being near him was going to kill her.

"Good day, then." She rose and dipped into a quick curtsey before leaving the room. Tears burned in her eyes, but she would never let him see it.

Jack put his head in his hands, elbows resting on his desk. She was crying, and it had taken every ounce of discipline he possessed to keep from running after her, to tell her he was only trying to force her hand, to make her admit that she loved him and that she believed him when he told her he had no desire to return to his life at sea. She was so afraid he might leave that she was denying them both what they wanted most.

Weary to the bone, and still aching from his accident in the park, he wished for a place he could find solace. Before, that place had always been aboard a ship, but he now found himself longing for the country estate on the coast. Even that would do him no good, however, if Ivy weren't with him.

He would never in a million years tie himself to a woman he didn't love and who didn't love him in return. He had already decided that when Sophia married and bore children, he would name one of them as his heir. The thought of trying to produce an heir with someone who was interested in his company only because he was wealthy and titled turned his stomach.

He had found his purpose, he acknowledged as he pinched the bridge of his nose to relieve the ache settling behind his eyes. He was devoted to caring for the tenants on his land and managing the property well with Fuddleston. He wouldn't be forced to waste his life in London trying to impress his peers. The country estate and other holdings he hadn't even visited yet needed him after years of his grandfather's neglect. The expressions of disbelief and gratitude on the faces of his tenants when he and Fuddleston had made their initial visits were burned into his memory, and he was humbled by their plight.

He heard the front door close behind Ivy, and he shut his eyes tightly. He would be forced to maintain his charade of looking for a bride if only to convince Ivy of what they both knew to be true. He would never give up. And Ivy Carlisle was no match for his determination. If it became apparent that she *was,* he supposed abduction was always an option. He smiled in spite of himself as he thought of her reaction to being trussed up like a Christmas goose and hauled into his carriage for a quick trip to Gretna Green.

Ivy prepared for the Norringtons' ball with a heavy heart. Standing before the long mirror in her dressing room, she assessed herself and knew she looked very pleasing on the outside. The shade of her dress matched her eyes to perfection, and her hair was piled beautifully atop her head in riotous curls shot through with strands of tiny pearls. Her maid had managed to arrange things just so and had even been able to hide the knot on her temple she'd received from the carriage accident.

She straightened her spine and placed a hand at her midsection, determined to be the social paragon she always had been. She supposed every young woman had fallen quite in love at one point or another. But practical was practical and reality was reality. And even though he seemed to have enjoyed her company, and certainly the kissing parts, she knew full well that she had made Jack batty with all of her rules and regulations. He would be better off with a woman who wouldn't hound him about propriety.

Ivy instructed her driver to take her first to Sophia's house, and she was genuinely delighted with her friend's stunning appearance. "Oh, mercy," she breathed as Sophia descended the stairway to the front hall. "Sophia, you are about to break many hearts."

"Psh," Sophia said, but Ivy noted a faint blush of pleasure cross her friend's features. "This old thing?"

"The lavender was the perfect choice." Ivy clasped Sophia's hands and leaned forward impulsively to kiss her cheek. She felt a bit foolish as her eyes burned with tears, and she laughed, clasping Sophia in an embrace. "You are a dear friend to me, Sophia, and I am so grateful for you."

She pulled back to see Sophia's eyes also shining, and Sophia shook her head. "Look at what you are doing to us, and on the night of my big debut!"

"Yes, quite right." Ivy sniffed as Sophia grinned and wiped a gloved finger at the corner of her eye.

"Ivy, before we leave, I must ask you something."

Ivy tipped her head in question as Sophia took a deep breath.

"I know you love my brother."

Ivy winced and felt her face flush.

"What I mean to say is that I know he loves you as well, and how often does such a thing come along? Please, won't you just . . . entertain the notion?"

Ivy softly let out a breath and turned her head, not wanting to meet the truth that was written on Sophia's face. "I'm certain it must seem foolish," she admitted quietly, "but, Sophia, he loves being at sea. He was nearly the captain of his own ship before all of this happened, and I couldn't bear to be the one who might keep him from his one true love. And I couldn't bear it if he left. As it is, I . . ." She shook her head.

"You?"

"I wonder if I should leave London for a time. He seems to finally have adjusted to the idea that he must marry, and he is rather looking forward to inspecting the flock tonight, I believe. I'm finding it much more difficult than I would ever have imagined to consider . . . it."

Sophia turned Ivy's gaze back to hers with a finger under the chin.

"Ivy, you are not leaving London. We have a girls' home to design and affairs to manage."

Ivy flushed. "Of course, I would never leave you to do it alone, I just . . . I don't know. My feelings are all a muddle."

Sophia smiled, and Ivy didn't like the look of it. "I'm certain they are." She linked her arm through Ivy's. "Come, let us fetch your darling Nana before the evening grows late."

Ivy's mother had been correct; the Norringtons' ball was an absolute crush, and Ivy was certain that Lady Norrington would be the talk of the *ton* for the remainder of the Season. The weather outside was splendid—neither too warm nor too cold—and the three sets of double doors leading off the ballroom to the back gardens were thrown open to invite a gentle breeze scented with lilacs and roses. It was the perfect evening for romance, and Ivy was absolutely dejected as she stood next to Sophia, Jack, and Lord Anthony Blake, who looked none too thrilled to be there himself. Ivy wondered why he had bothered make an appearance—perhaps he was finally going to heed his mother's wishes that he settle down.

"That one, you say?" Jack asked, motioning his glass of punch toward a group of giggling debutantes across the room. "The one in the center wearing pink?"

Ivy fought to keep from gritting her teeth. "Yes. Clarissa comes from a very suitable family, although the pink does little for her complexion, I must say."

Blake nudged Jack in the shoulder. "Perhaps if you ask, she'll let you inspect her teeth."

Jack snorted and grinned with Blake, who really was too handsome for words, Ivy thought with a scowl. He and Jack, standing side by side, were everything that was masculine and desirable and slightly roguish, which lent them both a lightly dangerous air that many a young woman would find appealing. Ivy wouldn't, of course, and she sniffed and turned her attention away from the pair who thought they were so clever.

Sophia took a sip from her punch and eyed Blake as well with one brow cocked. Ivy wondered if her friend had also noticed the charm the man exuded. It sparked a bit of interest that took Ivy's attention momentarily from her own pouting as she wondered if Sophia might be interested in Lord Blake. It certainly bore more reflection, and she tucked the thought away for later examination.

"Or Elizabeth Manning." Ivy caught Jack's attention with a slight tilt of her head toward a beautiful young woman with a head full of thick, blonde curls. "She is also very suitable, and her father is a marquess. She comes with a sizable inheritance, I understand."

Jack looked at Lady Elizabeth Manning and tipped his head to one side in apparent consideration.

"Eyes are a bit too big for her face, however," Ivy muttered under her breath and took a swig of her own drink as Sophia choked on hers.

Jack looked down at Ivy, and when she met his gaze, she very nearly dissolved into tears. "I'm sorry, I didn't hear you?" he said.

She shook her head. "It was nothing. You know, Jack," she said, setting her drink carefully on a passing server's tray, "you can have your pick of the lot. Any one of the single young women here is eligible and would make a lovely countess."

"I may have my pick of the lot, you say?"

She nodded stiffly and decided it was time she find Nana, who had gathered with some of her friends in the corner farthest from the orchestra, when she noted several heads turning in their direction, and she saw the unmistakable signs of women whispering behind their gloves.

"What . . ." she murmured and narrowed her eyes as she realized many of the people in the room were looking at Sophia.

"Blast," Ivy said under her breath. She knew the vicious bite of gossip when she saw it, and it was now directed full force at her friend.

CHAPTER 29

The bite of gossip can be painful, and one should make
every effort to abstain from participation in it!
Mistress Manners' Tips for Every-day Etiquette

W hat is it?" Jack whispered.

"I'm not certain." Ivy linked her arm with Sophia's and leaned over to her, whispering in her ear with a smile. "We are happy, and we are sharing the funniest of stories."

Sophia smiled and laughed with Ivy, looking for all the world as though she hadn't a care, but Ivy felt the tension running through her friend, and it made her angrier than she could ever remember feeling.

It was time for damage control. Ivy looked to the corner where Nana sat with her friends, only to see her grandmother making her way to their side of the room with Ivy's mother and father in tow. She straightened her spine, determined to defend the Elliots to her dying breath, even if it meant her own ruin. Perhaps she could move into the Elliot-Carlisle Home for Wayward Girls.

Ivy's mother approached with a winsome smile and extended both hands to Sophia, who disentangled her arm from Ivy's.

"My darling Miss Elliot," Ivy's mother said to Sophia loudly enough that several nearby clusters of gossip mongers couldn't help but hear, "it is so very good to see you again! And might I say it is just too bad of you to have visited only four times. You must come for tea tomorrow, for we have so much to discuss."

Ivy bit her lip to keep her mouth from falling open. Sophia had been introduced to her mother briefly at the funeral, but had certainly never visited them at the Carlisle home. Nana, who had arrived on Ivy's father's arm, leaned in to Ivy and whispered, "Lady Finster seems to have an issue with our dear Miss Elliot."

Ivy smiled at Nana and glanced around the room, seeing the venomous expression of Lady Finster, who stood near the opposite wall. She was looking at them with a murderous glare, and as Ivy glanced over the rest of the room, she saw the gossipers' expressions change from painful snickering scorn to surprise at the Carlisles' clear acceptance of the Elliots, to nods of approval.

Of course Lady Finster must have been in the wrong, they would all be saying to each other. The Carlisles held with only the very *best* of families—why, even their daughter's scandal could barely touch their good name!—and Lady Finster was well known to be spiteful anyway. And hadn't she been *bosom* friends with Mrs. Clista Elliot, who had tried to have the new earl *killed?*

As strains of music indicated the beginning of a new quadrille, Lord Anthony Blake made his way to Sophia's side and bowed low before her. "Might I be honored, Miss Elliot? I do hope this dance is not already spoken for."

Sophia smiled at him and curtseyed, handing Ivy her glass of punch and placing her hand in Lord Blake's. Her reputation was now fully protected. Blake's family was old, respected, and ridiculously wealthy, which counteracted his proclivities for putting on rakish airs. His mother would certainly not approve of him dancing with anyone less than worthy of the Wilshire title, so Miss Elliot *must* be up to snuff.

As they moved onto the dance floor, Ivy breathed a sigh of relief. "As scandals go, that was relatively quick," she murmured to Nana under her breath.

Ivy's mother straightened her cuffs and brushed at an invisible fleck of dust on her sleeve. "You spend inordinate amounts of time with the girl, Ivy," she said under her breath, "and it would hardly do for your name to be sullied because of an association."

Ivy's heart softened a fraction, and she looked closely at her mother. Gently clasping her forearms, she leaned forward and kissed her cheek. "Thank you, Mama," she said.

Lady Carlisle couldn't have looked more surprised had Ivy slapped her full across the face. She cleared her throat and nodded, looking decidedly uncomfortable. "Of course," she said stiffly, but Ivy noted the subtlest softening in her mother's expression, and she determined to be a bit more patient with her, express more warmth at home.

"I do not necessarily approve of this endeavor of yours," Lady Carlisle said with a sniff, regaining her perfect composure after throwing a quick glare at her mother-in-law, "however, I do suppose charity is a worthy endeavor, and so long as we have no scandal, I will not keep you from it."

She spoke of the girls' home, of course, and coming from Ivy's mother, this much was a vow of glowing support. Ivy nodded. "You will be most proud," she said.

"I find that I am already," Lady Carlisle said, and before Ivy could fully digest the compliment she'd been paid, her mother was off across the room at the excited bidding of one of her friends who was simply *dying* to show off her daughter's new gown.

"What's that?" Ivy's father said to a passing crony. "Yes, a drink would be just the thing. Mama, Ivy." He bowed and left them in favor of escaping the room, which grew more crowded with each passing moment.

" . . . how I ever produced such a dull child," Nana was saying, shaking her head at her son but wearing a reluctant smile.

Ivy's attention, however, was on Jack, who had nodded at her and was making his way across the room, apparently to ask for an introduction to Elizabeth Manning. She watched him move, with his easy grace and broad shoulders that slipped through the crowd as smoothly as he must navigate the movement of a rolling ship, and realized her chest positively ached. Drat it all, he had told her that she would be thinking of his kiss as he courted other women, and he'd been right. The thought of him kissing Elizabeth Manning had her wanting to claw that young woman's eyes out of her head.

Placing a hand to her heart, she wondered if it were possible to die from extreme emotion, and before she could disgrace herself with tears, she murmured a quick excuse to Nana and left the ballroom for the front hall.

Taking a few deep breaths, she chided herself soundly for behaving like such a ninny when she was getting what she wanted, after all. She had insisted that Jack see his family successfully launched into Society and find himself a bride. He was apparently more than halfway there, and she had nobody to blame but herself. He hadn't expressed his feelings for her again since returning from the coast, and she knew better than to hope for something that simply wouldn't be.

People continued to trickle in the front door, and Ivy was just wondering if she might be able to simply slip away unnoticed when Clarence Fuddleston entered, looking rather harried.

"Mr. Fuddleston!" Ivy rushed to his side and pulled him into the hall when the butler moved to bar the entrance. "What is it? Is it Mrs. Elliot?"

"What? No, no, Lady Ivy. It . . . well . . . I must speak with his Lordship."

Fuddleston respected well the rules of Society, and he would never have come to the ball if it weren't urgent. Ivy guided him to the small parlor to the right of the door and glanced inside, grateful to see it empty.

"I believe he is dancing, sir." Ivy frowned. "I know it is certainly none of my affair, but is it something to which I might be privy?"

Fuddleston nodded absentmindedly as though lost in thought, and he looked out at the hall full of people. "A stipulation," he said and reached into his pocket for a handkerchief, which he used to wipe his forehead. "I found a stipulation in the old earl's documents that allows for Jack—or rather, his Lordship—to return to a life of his choosing once he has successfully situated the estate affairs."

Ivy's mouth dropped open, and she stared at the small man. "How . . . where . . ." For a young woman who prided herself on articulation, it was a pitiful display.

Fuddleston shrugged, and Ivy realized the man looked quite miserable. "Buried in the main document, forty pages deep. Mr. Stallings wrote it, and I don't know that the old earl was even aware. Perhaps Stallings thought to use it to his own ends. But either way, his Lordship is free to go. I thought to tell him before he, well, he had mentioned something about a proposal, but if he is going to leave . . ."

The man looked at Ivy then, and she realized what a sad pair they must appear. Mr. Fuddleston had found a friend in Jack, and she was impressed with the fact that he was willing to show the discrepancy to Jack at all. He could very well have left it hidden with nobody the wiser.

Ivy drew herself up, eyes closed for a moment. "You are right to tell him, sir." She placed a hand on his arm, and he lightly covered it with his. After a gentle squeeze, he released her and quietly left the room.

Telling herself she had been right all along to try to protect her heart, Ivy waited alone for a few moments in the parlor before going back out to the hall and again into the ballroom. Fuddleston had hailed a servant, who made his way across the floor when the dance ended. Ivy could just see Jack through the crowd and then lost him again as people shifted and moved for the next dance.

There were too many people, too many dresses, too many drinks, too many fans, too much of everything except air, and Ivy felt nigh unto exploding. She tried to shove her way back out into the main hallway but found the egress thoroughly blocked. Turning around and dashing past Lord Hovley, who put a finger in the air as though to speak with her and then looked after her in bafflement, she wove through the throngs of people to the garden doors.

Once outside, she took a deep breath and bit her lip as her eyes brimmed with tears that she knew for certain she would no longer be capable of restraining. Rushing down the twisting path, she hurried past benches and romantic spots where a young couple might catch a moment to discreetly hold hands and whisper while an understanding chaperone turned the other way with a smile.

There was a gazebo—she and her mother had had tea with Lady

Norrington early in the Season outside in the shade of the charming structure, which was walled with climbing vines and lilacs and housed comfortable chairs with fluffy cushions. Desperately hoping nobody was in it, she ran up the steps and crossed the length of it, grateful beyond words to be alone.

She sank down on a bench and finally allowed her grief free reign. The sobs came hard, and she placed the back of her hand against her nose, her tears falling hot and soaking into the satin fabric of her glove. He would leave . . . of course he would. Why would he not? It was what he had always wanted.

And Ivy loved the sailor so much she feared her heart would break from it.

She lost track of time, immersed in her sorrow, shoulders heaving. When she felt someone place his hands on her arms, she gasped in surprise, pulling away reflexively.

"*Ivy,*" Jack murmured, not releasing her but pulling her closer instead. He was kneeling by the bench, his legs entwined in her skirts and his handsome face so very close to hers. "Ivy, you must stop." He placed his arms around her and pulled her against him.

"Then you should leave me alone," she cried against his chest, hating that he was witness to the most humiliating moment she could imagine. "Please, just leave." She clutched his shirtfront, tightening her fingers into fists until it hurt.

"Ivy, what is it?" He rubbed his hand slowly across her back and up to her neck, where he massaged gently with his thumb.

Sniffing and wiping her nose very inelegantly with her glove, she pulled back a bit and looked at him through blurred eyes, gratefully accepting the handkerchief he pulled from his pocket. "You," she said, sounding shaky and sad. "I . . . I . . ."

She looked past him as the dratted tears continued to fall, dully registering the fact that she would be beyond ruined if they were discovered. "Maybe I should plan on moving into the girls' home when it's finished," she said flatly and folded the handkerchief, again wiping her nose.

"What?" Jack laughed, and she glanced at him.

"My reputation will be in shreds if anybody—"

"I told your Nana to follow me." He gestured outside the gazebo with his head. "She's out there, protecting your virtue."

Ivy's lips twitched. "A fat lot she can do about it out there." She sniffed again. She took a deep breath and placed a hand at her waist, collecting herself and devising a plan to leave by skirting the house on the outside so she wouldn't have to traipse back through the ballroom.

Jack's hand against her cheek chased away all thoughts of escape as he caught her attention and, when she tried to look away, turned her back again. "Why are you out here crying as though your heart were broken?"

"My heart is broken." She cursed silently as her eyes filled yet again.

"Why?"

"You're cruel, you know. To force it from me is cruel."

"I need to hear you say it, Ivy."

She huffed as the tears fell down her cheeks anew. "I love you, Jack. You know that I do, and you are going to marry someone else or at the very least leave because now you truly can. Fuddleston is here, you know, with a message." Her heart tripped again at the memory of the solicitor's revelation.

Jack nodded. "I spoke with him. Just as I saw you making a mad dash out of the ballroom."

"So he told you, then. You're free to go."

Jack smiled at her and shook his head. "When are you going to believe me, Ivy Carlisle? I am not returning to the sea. It is a part of my life I will always appreciate, but I have work to do here: at the country estate with the tenants, and with you and Sophia and the home for wayward girls you apparently feel you might have to move into."

"Jack, I watched you in the maritime museum. You just . . ." she shrugged miserably, "you glowed when you spoke of it, of your dreams of commanding your own ship."

"There is much about that life that is less than wonderful, my sweet, but when I believed that such was my only course of action to support my family, it was enough. But now I have a different ship to command, and a much more compelling reason to remain on solid ground."

Ivy breathed out quietly, hardly daring to believe him. "Truly?"

He smiled and shook his head again. "Truly. Ivy Carlisle, I love you more than anything, and as I am here on bended knee, the time is opportune. Will you please, for the love of heaven, marry me?"

She sniffled and then smiled through the abysmal tears that she became convinced would never dry up. "Oh, Jack. Yes." She had hardly uttered the phrase when he captured her lips with his and kissed her until she couldn't breathe.

Pulling her close, his hand cradling her head to his chest, she heard him rumble, "Thank goodness. I thought I was going to have to dance another blasted quadrille with that girl whose eyes are too big for her face before you would come to your senses."

CHAPTER 30

*People are the most amazing of God's creatures; none
are to ever be discounted, for we may find ourselves
surprised at the value lying beneath the surface.*

Mistress Manners' Tips for Every-day Etiquette

I vy strolled through the art gallery, her arm in Jack's, looking at
Mary's pieces that were hung proudly on display. Nana had spon-
sored the exhibit, and the crowd was impressive; Ivy was gratified to
note that all but one piece had sold, and the showing had been under
way for less than an hour.

"Not that she needs it now to put food on the table, but your
mother could afford to dine on caviar and wine for the rest of her
days, if she chose. And this is but her first event." Ivy smiled up at
Jack and noted a fine sheen of moisture in his eyes that he blinked
back.

"I am so very proud of her." He placed his hand over Ivy's as they
continued to walk down the long hallway. "And of you," he added as
he squeezed her fingers.

Ivy blushed. Her advice column was in the editing stages

of becoming a book that was set to be printed within a couple of months. The unveiling of Mistress Manners' identity had come about unintentionally, but a correspondent at the magazine had let Ivy's name slip when turning in an interview he'd conducted with Ivy and Sophia regarding the progress of the girls' home. Word had spread like wildfire, of course, and Ivy had been relieved that rather than becoming the subject of scorn or condemnation, she was now regarded as something of an Original—Lady Olivia Knightley Carlisle's granddaughter, who taught the world how to behave and tamed a sailor in the process.

The banns had been posted, and Ivy and Jack were set to marry in two months' time. Her parents were thrilled, of course, and Sophia had the groom's family's responsibilities well in hand. She would be Ivy's maid of honor and had shed a tear or two when Ivy asked it of her.

"After the wedding," Jack said as they turned a corner and he steered her toward a door leading to a back garden, "I would like to leave London for a bit."

Ivy nodded. "Of course—I had assumed we'd go directly to the country estate after our trip to the continent."

"I am not looking to rush our trip, of course, but there is much to be done for the tenants, and furthermore," he said as he opened the door and followed her through it, "I find I do not want to share you with any more people than necessary."

Ivy blushed as he swept her into his arms and spun her to the corner of the building behind a large rosebush. He cut off anything she might have said as he leaned down with a grin and closed his lips over hers, and she wondered if there would ever come a day when she tired of that breathless feeling, the one that made her spine melt and her knees go weak.

When he finally let her up for air, trailing kisses along her jaw, she smiled. "And I find that I do not mind the thought of spending time with one handsome sailor."

"Or how about an earl?"

She laughed as he pulled her closer still. "Even better."

CHAPTER 31

A wedding is a time of celebration,
where loved ones gather with the couple to show support
and hearty felicitations. Cherish every moment.

Mistress Manners' Tips for Every-day Etiquette

Clarence Fuddleston watched the proceedings from a bird's-eye view. He stood between Lord Stansworth's other two grooms-men, Lord Anthony Blake and Master Pug Smith. The young boy occasionally stuck a finger inside his shirt collar and tugged a bit, but otherwise held up well in the new clothing Lady Ivy had insisted he be fitted for. The lady herself was resplendent in a gown made of material Fuddleston had no name for, and to her left stood Miss Sophia Elliot, looking equally resplendent in equally unnamable fabric.

The event was the rage of the Season, and everybody who was anybody was in attendance. If anybody thought it odd that the son of a disinherited earl would eventually inherit and then marry so well, he wisely kept it to himself. The Carlisles had closed ranks around Mrs. Mary Elliot, who sat in the congregation next to Lady Carlisle and looked markedly better in appearance than the first time Fuddleston had met her. She had put on some much-needed weight, and the coloring in her cheeks was becoming. He wouldn't be surprised to see her sought after by some nice elderly gentleman, but these days she was far too busy with her oils and canvases to take notice.

Fuddleston fought a ridiculous stinging in his eye at the sound of his employer's—his friend's—deep, resonating voice as he promised to love, honor, and cherish his bride. Fuddleston had never had a true friend in his life, and to now have one in the form of the kind, unconventional new earl was astounding and certainly nothing he had ever thought to experience.

As much as he'd thought the old earl a miserable, mean old man, and especially cruel to manipulate his grandson the way he had, Fuddleston was so grateful that he had found the courage that fateful night to enter Tilly's Tavern and seek out the rugged sailor, seated in the back and beating a man handily at cards.

It was the bravest and best thing Clarence Fuddleston had ever done.

ACKNOWLEDGMENTS

I wasn't sure this book would ever see the light of day, and I have many people to thank for the fact that it's now a reality.

To my agent, Pam van Hylckama Vlieg, you're a rock star.

To Lisa Mangum, Heidi Taylor, Chris Schoebinger, and Shadow Mountain as a whole, my heartfelt thanks for believing in me.

Thanks, as always, to the Bear Lake Monsters and the Goldenpens for the camaraderie and invaluable feedback.

And for their undying love and support, my gratitude goes to my family and in-laws. And to my husband, Mark, and for Nina, Levi, Anna, and Gunder. And Thor.

Discussion Questions

1. *My Fair Gentleman* is a twist on *My Fair Lady,* but instead of a flower girl being transformed into a lady, Jack is a sailor being transformed into a gentleman. In both stories, love plays a prominent role in the transformation. How has love transformed you?

2. Men and women played very different roles in Regency-era London. Discuss the gender roles and responsibilities of the era and how the story supports or subverts those roles. How have gender roles changed in our current society?

3. Olivia Knightly Carlisle is regarded as an "Original" by her family and society, which gives her an unusual measure of freedom for the era. What makes you an "Original"?

4. Society knows Ivy as a lady of society, but few know she is also the author of the Mistress Manners column. What dual roles do you play in your life? Do you have talents that you have kept secret from others?

5. Jack sets aside his personal ambition for the sake of his mother and sister, while Percival and Clista Elliot harbor much different ambitions for their family. Is ambition a positive or a

negative character trait? How does society perceive personal ambition? What are some of your personal ambitions?

6. Ivy's sister, Caroline, runs off with a man to whom she isn't married. Discuss how each member of Ivy's family reacts to Caroline's behavior. How does Caroline's actions affect Ivy's character development? How have the actions—good or bad— of a family member affected your own personal growth?

7. Select one of Mistress Manners' Tips for Every-day Etiquette and discuss if the advice still applies to today.

ABOUT THE AUTHOR

NANCY CAMPBELL ALLEN is the author of eleven published novels, which span genres from contemporary romantic suspense to historical fiction. In 2005, her work won the Utah Best of State award. She has presented at numerous writing conferences and events since her first book was released in 1999. Nancy received a BS in Elementary Education from Weber State University. She loves to read, write, travel and research, and enjoys spending time laughing with family and friends. She is married and the mother of three children.

A STEAMPUNK
PROPER ROMANCE

Beauty
AND THE
CLOCKWORK
BEAST

NANCY CAMPBELL ALLEN

When Lucy arrives at Blackwell Manor to tend to
her sick cousin, she finds that mysteries abound. A
restless ghost roams the hallways, and Lord Miles is
clearly hiding a secret. Working together, Miles and
Lucy attempt to restore peace to Blackwell Manor.
But can Lucy solve the mystery of Miles? Can she
love the man—beast and all?

August 2016

Paperback • 6x9 • 368 pages • $15.99
ISBN 978-1-62972-175-0

Learn more at ShadowMountain.com

SHADOW
MOUNTAIN